For Troy Slater
of Glenwood High School
Glenrothes, Fife

Seriously Weird

Chapter One

Number One, Number One
Now my song's just about begun –

It was Pupil-Free day at school – you know, the one where the kids don't go to school while the teachers do and have a ball without us telling them what to do. I wonder what they do do without us. Sing? Dance? Have a gig? A thrash? A feast? Play cards? W-O-R-S-E?

Anyway, this led to the usual talk with Mum. We've been there, done that, said that, over and over again.

'Claire!'

'Yes, Mum?'

'I'll be in the morning, but I have to go out in the afternoon.' Mum has a part-time job in a supermarket which she doesn't think much of – she's trying to write children's stories so she can pack it in. Dad doesn't think much of *them*. 'So I'll need you to stay in with Troy.'

'Oh, Mum! My friends are going ten-pin bowling and I want to go with them!'

'Take Troy with you . . .'

'NO! He'd wreck it!'

'Bring your friends here, then.'

'No way. Can't Ness do it?'

Vanessa's my older sister and at the Sixth Form college.

'No. She's working this afternoon.'

3

'Huh – she would.'

'Look, you go out in the morning with your friends. How about swimming? I'll fund you. Then stay in this afternoon while I go out.'

'OK. Maybe. But I'll miss the ten-pin bowling. An' I wanted that.'

'I'll make it up to you. And I'll tell Troy not to play up.'

'Oh, he's OK with just me. It's just I wanted. . . Never mind, it's OK, OK.'

We live in Thorneycroft Crescent – about twenty neat semi-detached houses with neat gardens opposite each other with a turning at the end round a pretty little island with a tiny wood on it, and lots of thorny bushes and flowers growing round them. If you're tough enough to get through the thorns there's a green oasis in the middle. I used to go there often when I was little. My brother Troy still does. And set back from the Crescent is a big, very old sixteenth-century pub with beams and everything. It's got a garden, an adventure playground and a ghost – yeah, a real live ghost – no, I mean a real, dead one. They've painted a ghost looking out of one of the windows, quite spooky, it is. But the real one hasn't been seen lately, maybe put off by the painted ghost, or by Troy, my brother, living near. Behind the pub are woods and fields and a river below a wooded hill and on the other side there's our school on a level playing field, a modern smart school. All the houses are freshly painted and smart. Shining cars are parked neatly in the garages or on the hard-standings, rows of shiny insects.

And us? Yeah, we're there! Number 13. Did somebody say 'Unlucky for some'? We're the Spiers family, Mum (Julie), Dad (Jack), Vanessa (Ness), beautiful, clever and musical, yuck, what more don't you want in an elder sister? Me, Claire, fat, ordinary, nice (I hope), Bowie the dog and Troy, my brother. He's called Troy because Dad and Mum argued over his name, Mum wanted Tom (her dad), Dad wanted Roy (his dad). They argue over nearly everything but in the end settled on Troy – nothing to do with Greeks and wooden horses. And afterwards – they went on arguing over Troy. For ever and ever.

Then Ma Haynes came over from next door, number 14, the house joined to ours, pushing open the door and walking right in as she does.

'Can you have Morris for the day? I've got to work and I expect you're free.'

Ma Haynes thinks she's the only one who ever does any work.

Bowie came out of his basket and barked at her. He hates her, though not as much as Dad does, interfering old bag, he says. She stepped back as Bowie shoved his face at her. He's got hundreds of big teeth.

'Can't you shut that dog up? He'll do someone some damage . . .'

'Claire, put Bowie outside.'

Out went Bowie into the back garden. He didn't want to go into the back garden, tough, Bowie, but we can't have you biting Ma Haynes.

'Funny name for a dog!'

'I've told you, Mrs Haynes. It's because he's got one brown eye and one blue one. Like David Bowie,' I said.

'Who's he? Oh, don't bother to tell me. He's a funny-looking dog. I'm surprised you keep him, with his nasty temper an' all. I'd've thought you'd got enough on your plate with your Troy, without having a wall-eyed dog as well.'

'A what?'

'Wall-eyed. It's what they call funny dogs with odd eyes.'

Oh, I hate her, I thought.

'He's a lovely dog! And he's not nasty-tempered. Only with *some* people.'

'Would you like a cup of coffee, Marjorie?' interrupted Mum quickly. 'And hurry up, Claire, your friends are probably waiting for you.'

'No, thank you,' said Mrs H. 'I haven't come to stay. Only to ask if you can have Morris for the day? He'll be no trouble to you. A well-behaved boy, he is.'

'No, he can't come,' came a voice from the under-the-stairs cupboard, where Troy had gone to ground when he heard her. 'I'm working on my new project and I don't want Molly here. I don't want Molly anywhere.'

Molly is what they call Morris Haynes at school. Ma Haynes took no notice.

'He can play with your Troy,' she smiled at Mum.

'No, he can't,' cried the voice-under-the-stairs.

'Troy can be awkward,' Mum said slowly. She made no effort to make him come out. She knew it would be a waste of time.

6

'Oh, Morris doesn't mind. And *we* all know that Troy isn't as bad as people say. They'll get on like a house on fire!'

That's all we need, I thought, Molly and Troy in a house on fire. I ran out of the door, feeling free, off to join *my* friends, my crowd, Kim, Abby, Beth and Lily. Kim's my oldest, my best friend, black and beautiful, Beth's new, Abby – mm – Abby comes and goes, and Lily's shy and Chinese. They look after me when it's tough. They're friends. With my life, I need friends.

Mum was smiling and humming a horrible retro song when I got back. And I wondered if she used to be happy like that before Ness and Troy and mortgages turned her and Dad into sad people. Specially Troy. We've got a photograph of her and Dad sitting on a bank laughing. She looks about fifteen and really pretty. Troy looks like her.

'What a beautiful child,' people say. 'Those eyes! That hair!'

He's got dark brown eyes, yellow and brown stripy hair and a little flat nose. He looks like a tiger cub.

'Yeah,' Dad grins, 'only tigers are better-looking.'

Once Ness decided he was an alien. She found a story about one who kept wishing people he didn't like into a graveyard.

'Shut up. Don't be horrible,' I cried. But maybe she was right. She can't be, though, can she? Troy is OK, isn't he? I often wonder. We all do.

'I'm sorry to leave them both with you,' said Mum, 'but I had a word with Troy and he promised – you know – to behave. I think he listened. They played on the PlayStation and we've walked Bowie to the shops . . .'

'I thought Molly . . .'

'Don't call him Molly. It's not fair. How would you like being called Molly if you were a boy?'

'I wouldn't. But *he's* called Molly 'cos he's a wimp.'

'Claire!'

'What I was going to say was I thought he was scared of Bowie. Suppose Bowie goes for him?'

'Troy talks to Bowie and he'll be all right with Morris.'

'Huh, the Dog-Whisperer now, is he? We can make a film about him. Bring your mad dogs to Troy Spiers and he'll sort them out whispering down their ears. That's because he's mad as well.'

'Claire!'

'Stop saying "Claire", Mum. I've given up ten-pin bowling which Kim's Mum had booked for me with the others so don't expect me to be a saint as well. Mum?'

'Yes?'

'Do you think he'll always be like this?'

'Sometimes he's fine.'

'Yeah. Sometimes.'

'You're a good girl, Claire. Don't know how I'd manage without you.'

'Save the halo for later. I might just need it. And go, Mum. We'll be OK.'

Back at home, knackered after all the swimming, I plonked down on a sofa with a book to watch a video. I like reading a bit and watching a bit, and follow them both at once. And I'd got a bar of chocolate out of my secret hiding place – no way do I tell anyone where it is. But I must've fallen asleep because I woke up with a twitch. Eh? What's going on? My sixth sense had switched on, I knew something was up. I wish I could switch it off. But I can't with Troy about. Neither can Mum. Ness can switch off. So can Dad, sometimes.

'Oh, Clarry, go back to sleep.' When I'm talking to myself, I'm always Clarry to me. You know what I mean. Claire sounds so cool and smooth, like a looking-glass, so I don't talk to her. Sometimes she doesn't seem to be me, but like frozen Arctic roll. Clarry's warm and funny and streetwise and clever. I hope. Not me, really. Yes, she is. A bit.

'Troy isn't the only one crazy in your family,' said Kim when I told her about Clarry. But Clarry was listening now as well as Claire.

For in the next room Molly was squeaking on and on and on. Like a dripping tap or rain in the jungle, drip, drip, drip. He's called Molly at school because he's a creep, a wimp and a whinger. He moans, he whines, he tells tales, everything he does is someone else's fault. We get told to be nice to him, make space for him, and we try, but he always, always gripes at us and tells tales and lies about us to the teacher. And, yes, we are sorry for him, he's so awful. But it's not easy. And he likes to tell you what *you* ought to do. And what not to do. He likes to mind your business for you as well as his own.

'You shouldn't do that, Troy,' he was saying.

No reply. I was wide awake now listening to the

moan, whine, drip, moan, whine, drip. Not a peep, not a murmur was coming out of Troy. What was he doing?

'That was naughty. Swearing's naughty.'

Listening to Molly was like being at one end of a telephone conversation.

'You're not allowed to do that.

'That was naughty. You'll be punished.

'My mother says it's very wrong to say those rude words. And spit. And pull those horrible faces.

'I want to go home.

'I don't like you, Troy Spiers. I wanted to like you, but I don't.

'What were you writing out all those numbers for? You're always writing out numbers. You nutty or somethin'? Nutty about numbers, ha, ha. Geddit?

'Why don't you play a proper game? With me.

'I'll tell your mother about you. And my mother.

'That's a horrible dog. Why have you got such a horrible dog? He's growling at me.

'Why are you so horrible, Troy Spiers?

'My mother said you'd got to play with me. And all you've done is write out numbers and play your football game that I don't understand. I don't want to be in your house, Troy Spiers.

'Mummy said you're a naughty boy and your Dad ought to give you a good hiding or you'll end up in prison when you grow up.'

Clarry was telling Claire she'd better do something. So I went into the front room. Troy's football pitch was scrunckled all over the floor, players lying higgledy-piggledy, some broken. Torn pieces of paper with numbers on lay round about.

'I didn't mean to do that, Troy. But you went off somewhere and I was bored. Don't look like that, Troy. I won't ever do it again. I'm sorry, Troy. I don't like that dog, Troy.'

The dog didn't like Morris either. Snarling quietly, he was resting his snout on his paws, watching, watching, waiting.

Suddenly Troy charged out of the room and up the stairs, stopped at the top and stood holding the newel post, breathing hard.

'Just leave him alone, Morris,' I said. But Morris had never left anything alone in the whole of his yucky life. He went out the room, too.

Tiger-faced Troy watched Molly follow him up the stairs.

'Come with me, Morris,' I called. 'We'll go in the garden.' He took no notice.

Troy waited, eyes wild, like Beethoven in a rotten temper, thinking up a new symphony using different notes and strange instruments. This could only mean trouble. And I didn't want trouble. I wasn't sure I could cope.

'Stop it!' I yelled, but it came out a squeak.

Molly was nearly at the top, panting a bit. Like a lioness watching her kill, a fox watching a rabbit, a cat watching a bird, Troy waited.

'Be nice, Troy. I said I'm sorry.'

Nice? How could Troy be *nice*? Being *nice* and Troy were nothing to each other; chalk, cheese, water, oil. Troy could be brave, clever, stupid, quicker than lightning, funny, even kind (occasionally), mad (often), but NICE? Do you ask a cheetah or a computer to be *nice*?

He waited at the top of the stairs as Morris came up to him. Bowie slinked past Morris and lined up behind Troy, who waited at the top of the stairs Mum had stripped to the bare wood, sick of the old carpet, she'd said.

'Dangerous like that,' Gran had sniffed. 'You'll need a thick soft rug at the bottom.'

'Now you be a good boy, a friend,' and Molly held out a hand. 'And I won't tell your mother about you.'

I ran to the bottom of the stairs.

'Stop it, you two!' I cried. 'Right now!' But they were deep into their warfare and didn't hear me.

Morris tried to get up beside Troy, who ignored the outstretched hand, his dark eyes brilliant like stars, stripy yellow hair standing on end.

Clarry knew what he was going to do. But Claire couldn't stop him. Troy put both hands on Molly's chest and pushed. Hard, hard as he could and Morris screamed as he fell down the shining, newly stained wood. I was screaming too,

'No, no, no, no. Oh, Troy!'

I stretched out my arms as wide as possible as Morris fell down, down, down, on top of me. We landed together in a heap, Morris flattening me.

I was the thick, soft rug at the bottom. I might have guessed.

Ma Haynes and Mum burst into the hall together.

'Morris!' shrieked his mum.

'What on earth are you doing with Morris in your arms at the bottom of the stairs?' shrieked mine.

'Troy pushed me. Troy pushed me. He could've killed me!' Morris wailed piteously, clutching his mum.

'That wicked boy! I'll do him for this!' shouted Ma Haynes. 'He could've killed darling Morris. Oh, my boy!'

She pulled him up and they sobbed together.

'Where's Troy?' asked Mum, helping me up, but looking round wildly. 'Where's Troy. Where's he gone?'

'Morris, are you hurt? Have you broken anything?'

I shouted, 'Mum, I nearly got killed. Are you listening? Morris almost flattened me. MUM!'

'Where's Troy?'

'Show me where it hurts, Morris darling!'

'Tell me where Troy has gone, Claire. And the dog. What happened?'

Nobody asked if I was hurt. Nobody cared twopence about me. I might as well not have been there. They only cared about their HORRIBLE SONS!

'Morris was a pain. Troy got mad. End of story,' I said. Sulking.

'Where is he now?'

Her face was anguished and I can't really be cross with my mum, so: 'I know where he'll be. And Bowie.'

Limping, I led Mum down the road, while Mrs Haynes and Morris went home shouting about suing us for damages. Clarry muttered silently that Claire was the

13

only one damaged so why didn't she shut up?

We went to the island at the end of Thorneycroft Crescent with its tiny wood full of thorn bushes (I reckon that's how it got its name) and crept inside. Sometimes Troy hides there when life gets a bit much. Mum hadn't been in there before. She squeaked a bit and moaned, but kept going.

Bowie was sitting up alert, on guard for Troy who was lying flat out scribbling numbers in a scruffy exercise book.

'What have you done now?' cried Mum. She looked terrible – red eyed with leaves in her hair, scratches on her arm. Me, I ached all over. I'd be covered in bruises by tomorrow.

'What have I done? I dunno, Mum. Look, now this is really interesting, the way these two sets of numbers work out here. I got it at last. Have a look, Mum! See? Isn't it great?'

Chapter Two

Write down the number 9 (Troy's age)
Write down the multiples of 9: 18 27 36 45 54 63 72 81 90
Add all the numbers together to get 495
Add the digits together: $4 + 9 + 5 = 18$
Add digits together: $1 + 8 = 9$. The answer is always 9.

I must have been about six when I really realized Troy was different. I think it was one day when he sat on a wet pavement in front of the fire station's yellow hydrant signs and refused to be shifted. Four over five, he kept murmuring, four over five, lovely, lovely. Over and over and over. He screamed horribly as Mum and I tried to drag him away and a policeman came up to ask what we were doing to the little boy and some woman said that cruel people like my mother didn't deserve to have children. Quite a crowd gathered before we could get away with Troy, smiling at last in his buggy, Mum white-faced and me shouting. He did this with all the hydrant signs in town.

Yet Mum still wouldn't listen to us when we said he was crazy, mad, nutty, barmy.

'It's only 'cos he's a boy. Boys are different. Boys will be boys,' she'd murmur proudly as he did something awful. Again.

'Mum,' Ness shrieked. 'There was a woman's movement or hadn't you noticed? You're stuck in the dark ages! You can't let boys get away with *murder* just because they've got willies!'

'Don't let me hear you talking like that. You two are very naughty, unkind girls. Jealousy, that's what it is!'

'God give me strength to cope with barmy mothers,' Ness shouted. 'What hope is there with you around? Listen, Troy is great, super – but he's BARMY! Take him to see the doctor.'

'I don't want to listen to you any more, Vanessa. Go up to your room and stay there. And stop pulling faces in the mirror, Claire, and get the washing up finished. You talk about Troy, but you're a bit funny sometimes.'

Ness stormed off upstairs. I was going to answer back, but my mother's so little and worried all the time I can't go at her like Ness does. I just did the washing up and played one of Troy's football number games with him in case he'd heard and his feelings were hurt, though why bother? He never listens to anything he doesn't want to.

So it went on, screams in the bank and the post office – tins knocked flying in the supermarket. In the end I just had to wait outside with him while Mum went in. He yelled if Mum stopped to talk to anyone, he never knew anybody till he'd met them six or seven times and he spat, kicked or swore at anybody he didn't like, which was nearly everybody. But Mum was thrilled when he could count to a hundred at age two and knew all his tables at three.

'He'll astonish us all,' she smiled proudly.

'I can't wait. The suspense is killing me,' Dad groaned. Only Ness laughed.

Mum insisted on sending him to the Sunday School. Everyone told her this was a waste of time, but she only said how much she'd loved it when she was little and she was sure Troy would love it, too. I had to go with him, of course, and listen to him singing 'One, Two, Three, Four, Five, Once I caught a fish alive,' over and over at the top of his voice when they were practising for the carol concert. Mum was asked not to send him again.

'I can't understand people,' she said, as complaints rolled in from neighbours, parents, friends and teachers as he fought, spat, kicked and swore his way through home, Thorneycroft Crescent and school. Kids called him Vesuvius because he erupted like a volcano.

Water was the other thing – he loved water. He'd look at moving water for hours. Once he sat on a rock in a river – the river behind the pub – and watched the water tumbling over the rocks for three hours. Dad got soaked getting him off in order to go home.

I think Dad was very patient, though he did say he hadn't thought being a parent meant guerrilla warfare all the time and have all the neighbours hating him.

Troy also liked football, not to play, in fact he was dangerous to the other players when let loose on the pitch, but he liked watching the scores come in on Saturday. It was the numbers connection that he liked, I think. Anything to do with numbers.

Sometimes Troy was fine. One or two little girls in his class he actually liked and they looked after him, sorting his books and pens and fixing his trainers and eating his school dinners for him to save him from getting into trouble *all* the time. You see he only ate baked beans and he liked them best in the tin. And Ricicles for breakfast. It had to be Ricicles. He wouldn't eat any other cereal. And he hated eating with other people. If he ever had to have roast dinner he drove us crazy by counting all the peas or potatoes. Or he'd lay out his chips like soldiers and sing number songs to them.

He built things at home, castles, forts, patterns, space stations, using Lego, shells, leaves, blocks of wood, stone, pebbles, brick, and he screamed and roared every time you knocked them over or trod on them – like every day, for they were always in the way. And he scribbled all over the house . . .

'Boys do,' Mum smiled proudly.

I wasn't allowed to scrawl everywhere, but Troy's numbers and diagrams appeared all over the place. You can grow to hate hexagons and the times tables. At last Dad decorated once more and said this time the walls had to stay clean or else. This was fine.

'You only need to tell him reasonably,' my mother said. 'See, he's stopped writing all over the walls.'

That didn't last long, though. Not with Troy.

Sometimes I got fed up. Ness was the eldest, very pretty and clever. She did just as she liked, too. She got away with murder. Mum was really proud of her. But me – she seemed to think I'd been put on the planet to look after Troy. If she couldn't read him a story at night, I had to. He liked stories he knew well, best if they'd got numbers in them, and he'd hit me if I got a word wrong. I always had to help her with him, give up what I was doing if she thought he needed me.

One day, not long ago, Clarry came into the mirror when I was looking at it to see if I'd got a bruise where Troy had hit me when I wouldn't play one of his games with him. I looked different and I saw it was my other half, the one who lived in my head and sometimes in my tum if things were awful. *Hi, Claire*, she said, *I'm Clarry* – and I knew SHE wasn't a sad wimp doing everything for everybody else and not having a rebel self. She said what I wanted to say. She was clever and sharp and *brave*.

And so that's how we were, me and Clarry.

Dad worked for a computer firm, a job he didn't like, and was always saying he wanted to do something else, though he never said what. Mum had a part-time job in the supermarket and wrote kids stories, when she could. She was going to make us all rich, she hoped. She insisted on reading them to Dad, who didn't think much of them.

'They're awful,' he said. 'Kids don't like fairies and toadstools and magic swords any more. Look at 'im,' he jerked a thumb at Troy who was busy with one of his football games – *Convicts & Crooks vs. Prison Warders*. He's got loads of these including a cricket game that seems to involve the whole world.

'Kiddies love fairies, don't they, Troy?' Mum pleaded.

'One million and nine hundred thousand,' he replied. 'Fairies are crap!'

Chapter Three

Ten green bottles hanging on the wall
Ten green bottles hanging on the wall
And if one green bottle should accidentally fall
There'd be nine green bottles hanging on the wall
(. . . up to) One green bottle hanging on the wall, etc.
There'd be no green bottles hanging on the wall.

Saturday and noises, voices shouting and complaining, bangs, knocking on the door, ringing on the bell, feet running and shuffling, things GOING ON – right under my bedroom window from the sound of it. Something UP – something UP down there in the street below my window.

Trouble, trouble, trouble. I knew it 'cos Clarry and my sixth sense were telling me . . . trouble, trouble, trouble.

Git up, you bone-idle git, Clarry, my other half, was muttering from some place in my middle or wherever she hangs out. Sometimes warm, funny Clarry turns into a streetwise pain-in-the-arse know-it-all and tells me what to do, running my life for me, telling me to slim and sort myself out. Sometimes I hate Clarry.

'Don't want to.' I slid down under the duvet. 'I'm staying here all day, so there. Somebody else can get up and look.'

The noises outside were growing louder. I just couldn't

stay hiding under the duvet.

Clarry said, *Get up, Claire. Join it.*

So I pushed my feet out, padded over to the window and pulled open the curtains.

It was a beautiful morning. Summer coming and out of a clear blue sky the sun shone down on the flowers and the trees in blossom . . . and on people gathering outside our house and down our path and up the steps to the front door. Angry people, shouty, bangy, red-faced, cross people, rage people.

I went into Ness's room.

'Nessa,' I called. 'Come and look.' She didn't move.

I went over and shook her. She grunted like a little pig and snuggled herself under the bedclothes. I flung back her duvet. She moaned feebly. I dragged her to the window.

'See.'

The pavements, the road and the parked cars were covered with numbers, diagrams and symbols.

'Bring him out here! Make him clean it up,' shouted a voice.

'Oh, heck,' moaned Ness. 'Why didn't he just write "Troy was here" over everything. I'm going back to bed. I don't want to be lynched by the mob.'

As she shot back and under her duvet the doorbell was ringing non-stop.

I heard a bolt draw back, a door open.

'What's – what's the matter?' My mum's voice sounded nervous and I hate my mum being scared.

I dragged on my denim jacket over my jams and leapt

21

downstairs three steps at a time. 'Shut it, Clarry, I'm on my way,' I told the commentator in my middle and:

'Mum, I'm coming. Don't worry. I'm coming,' I called.

But Dad had got there first. Moving Mum out of the way as if she was a bit of nothing, he filled the doorway.

He didn't speak. Just stood there. In Mum's lime-green velvet dressing gown grabbed in a hurry. She's a little woman and he's a big man. The dressing gown didn't cover him. If he wasn't my dad I'd say he was scary. The crowd fell back a bit, then warmed up again.

I knew what it was all about. I didn't need Clarry telling me. Troy had moved out of our house and was carrying out his favourite project in Thorneycroft Crescent. He's got lots but this is the one he always comes back to:

Start with a 1 (one)	1 (one)
Double it to 2	Halve it to $1/2$
Double 2 making 4	Halve this to $1/4$
Double 4 making 8	Halve this to $1/8$
Double 8 to 16	Halve $1/8$ to $1/16$
Double 16 to 32	Halve $1/16$ to $1/32$
Double 32 to 64	Halve $1/32$ to $1/64$
Double 64 to 128	Halve $1/64$ to $1/128$
Double 128 to 256	Halve $1/128$ to $1/256$

And so on infinitum. He loves it. No, don't ask why.

Funny, really. I first showed this to Troy when he was really little and still taking his abacus to bed with him, counting the beads to the tune of one, two, three, four, five.

I liked the way it matched but I always gave up at 256 1/256. As anyone sane would. But Troy isn't sane.

He's bonkers, barmy, crazy, nuts, seriously weird. What Troy wants to do is to see if you can carry it on for ever and ever to infinity.

Our lives are filled with numbers going to infinity. Everywhere. That's what we live with, why Mum is nervous all the time and Dad has a temper like a lion with toothache. Only last week Mum said she was glad that at least he'd stopped drawing all over the house. No more numbers down the hall. No more hexagons in the bathroom. A newly decorated room could stay decorated, hooray. He was cured.

But he wasn't. He'd just moved out of our house into the street, Thorneycroft Crescent. He'd taken the numbers etc. with him.

And the neighbours were at the door, just like those mob violence crowds on telly.

'Look, look,' screeched Ma Haynes. 'See what he's done! Now you've *got* to do something!'

'I don't care if he has got a Beautiful Mind,' shouted Creep Matt Taylor, dumped by Vanessa about a month ago and hating us all ever since. 'That's no reason for him to do his rotten drawings all over my old man's car.'

'Excuse me.'

Mr Fortescue-Corbett had arrived. Big executive man, big executive house on the corner of Thorneycroft Crescent, one up on the neighbours, big executive suit, big executive briefcase, big executive car now covered with triangles and circles, and the nine times table.

'Spiers,' he said – that's my dad. 'Spiers, what is the meaning of this?'

'Of what?' asked my Dad. 'Anything wrong?'

Mr Fortescue-Corbett spluttered a bit.

'Haven't you got eyes, man? Can't you see?'

'See what?'

'All this . . . horrible graffiti? All over my car? In the crescent?'

'I don't think it's graffiti . . .'

'Then what is it? Your ill-disciplined lout has totally wrecked this street. And if you don't get this cleaned up, I'll send for the police.'

'Yes, send for the police,' called out Ma Haynes and several others. 'Send for the police.'

Mr Fortescue-Corbett pushed up to Dad, him in his executive suit, my dad in Mum's dressing gown, earrings and bare feet. They stood eyeball to eyeball. Not road rage – Troy rage – we knew it well.

'You needn't bother. Troy'll clean it up,' said Dad and –

'Get him,' he hissed at me.

'Yes, Dad,' I said, leaping up the stairs, a kangaroo on speed, followed by Mum, and shoved open Troy's door. Troy was still asleep. He looks like a Botticelli cherub when he's asleep. We stood looking at him. A tear slid down Mum's face.

When she pulled back his bedclothes he was still in jeans and T-shirt.

'Up all night,' he yawned. 'Lovely numbers in the moonlight.'

'Oh, Troy,' was all my mother could or would say as we walked him down the stairs.

'It's gonna be awful down there,' I whispered in his

ear. 'Don't be scared. But you *are* an idiot.' He took no notice.

A roar went up when he appeared.

'Clean it up, you wicked boy.'

'You'll go to prison, Troy Spiers,' Molly Haynes called out.

Mum was gathering buckets, mops, sponges, sprays.

'Don't worry, it'll come off easily. Claire will help,' she cried.

Claire the skivvy, Cinderella Claire, Fat Claire, Ugly Sister Claire, only one ugly here, yeah, that's me.

Our neighbours went on yelling and it was not a pretty sound.

'Troy, the hose round the side of the house. Go and get it, Claire,' said Dad.

Clarry told me I was a wimpish git as I unwound the hose, a very long one. But why should I be the one to get it?

'Get out of the way, everybody,' Dad ordered. 'He'll do ours and then if you get your hoses ready he'll clean yours up, won't you, Troy. Let's all get going and sort it out. And move it! Mr Fortescue-Corbett has to get to the airport.'

But Mr Fortescue-Corbett's mouth had fallen open. Ness, wearing her new nearly transparent turquoise harem pyjamas that show off her ruby belly-button ring and more beside, had joined us on the steps. Clarry hissed to me that she'd somehow found time to brush her hair, which flowed around like a . . . like a . . . I dunno what, but there was a lot of it. Her feet were bare and her

25

toenails painted gold and scarlet. If Troy looked like a cherub she looked like an angel.

She's been busy, Clarry muttered.

Troy spotted me with the hose and grabbed it. You see, if there's something else he's crazy about besides *numbers* it's water. He's nuts about water. He switched on the hose button and lovingly he sprayed the hose on full power straight into the mouth and face of Mr Fortescue-Corbett standing there staring goggle-eyed and gobsmacked at Ness.

Then high and wild with the glory of a hose on full power, he waved it round and round in a circle. As I heard the screams I looked at Dad. He had a tiny grin at the corner of his mouth just before he grabbed the hose back off Troy. If my brother's mad (and he is) then I know who he gets it from.

Later, after we'd cleaned it all up, Mum and me (helped by Kim and friends) spent Sunday printing sorry, sorry, sorry cards and delivering them. We couldn't get Troy to sign so we forged his signature.

Oh, and Ness brought home a new boyfriend.

That one's dishy, said Clarry.

'Shut up,' I answered. 'Why should I care?'

Chapter Four

Troy's Dice Cricket Game

Two dice. ⚀, ⚁, ⚂, ⚃ and ⚄ are runs. ⚅ is out or lose a life.

Two ⚅s = out.

Alternating Batsmen: Nos 1–4 three lives 5–7 two lives 8–11 one life.

Team with most runs wins.

Two innings.

The sea sparkled, bluer than blue, with shimmering white lines, boats with red and blue sails moving on the water. Swimmers' heads bobbed up and down in the water. It was Enid Blyton Adventure Time – sun – sea – cliff – caves. Seaside holidays for ever.

We were staying at Gran's who lives by the sea, lucky Gran. Been retired here yonks. Said she was going to build sandcastles in her old age. Grandad died (or ran away) years ago – I'm never quite sure which – and there she lives with her cat Eric, always ready to make us welcome when Thorneycroft Crescent gets a bit much. You see, Troy doesn't bother her at all. He's the image of his Grandad, she says, and Great-Uncle Tom who was completely bonkers till he finally left for a faraway island in Sweden. I think he's still there, she says. He was apparently crazy as a kid, so what with Grandad and Great-Uncle Tom, Gran is quite used to nutters. She says Troy is perfectly OK if you just leave him alone and it's true she never gets any trouble from him.

We'd come for half-term as we weren't exactly Flavour of the Month in Thorneycroft Crescent. Most of the chalk had gone by now, mainly because me and my friends had helped Mum scrub them out with mops, sponges and anything you can think of.

But no one in the Crescent was speaking to us. And somebody had pinned a flyer with 'Try Emigrating. Australia Needs You. We Don't', on our door.

So I rang up Gran, who rang up Mum, saying she fancied seeing us and why didn't we stay with her for a few days.

Why not? Dad said. Troy might as well wreck St Dunstan's-by-the-Water as anywhere else. Can she manage Bowie as well? Ness wanted to bring her new boyfriend Adam as she was being stalked, she was sure, by Matthew Taylor, and Mr Fortescue-Corbett kept drawing up beside her in his Merc and asking if she needed a lift anywhere.

So, the following Saturday morning we all set off, with Ness and Adam, the new boyfriend, following in his car – a better one than ours as he's posh and rich.

She wouldn't have anyone who wasn't, mutters Clarry and I try to think that's a nasty thing to say about your sister. *Don't make me laugh*, answers Clarry. *You know Ness*. Now Mum just says *she's* grateful to anyone who'll play with Troy. At first, when Adam came round . . .

'Who's that?' he asked. We told him. Troy taught him his favourite cricket game.

'He's OK,' Troy said at the end, 'though I don't know why she wants a boyfriend when she's got me.'

Ness lifted her eyes to the ceiling. 'Retard,' she murmured.

'Stop it,' Mum cried, furious.

Adam turned up the next day.

'Hi, Troy.'

'Who are you?'

'Adam. Remember?'

'Never seen you before. Who are you?'

'Vanessa's boyfriend. Well, at least I hope I am, if she'll let me be.'

'You don't want to snog with her. That's boring. Oh, I know. I showed you my cricket game. You've got to play with me. Don't bother with Ness.'

Adam nobly played cricket till Vanessa came out with, 'If you don't stop playing that crappy game and come out with me, I'll text Matthew Taylor . . . and . . .'

'OK, OK, OK, Vanessa. Sorry, Troy. I've got to go.'

He managed to get through the door just in time to avoid one of Troy's trainers hurled at him. After a few more evenings Troy recognized Adam when he saw him and they'd play a game before Adam and Vanessa went clubbing or whatever.

'He's such a nice boy,' smiled Mum happily. 'Troy likes him!' If Troy likes anyone they're tops with Mum. So Adam was invited to come to St Dunstan's-by-the-Water as well.

It was great to get away from the grey cloud of Thorneycroft Crescent where nobody was speaking to us, but looking the other way when we met them. St Dunstan's blazed with flowers and wonderful whoopsy sunshine, candyfloss, ice-creams, bouncy castles, adventure parks, miniature golf and the sea, the sea, the sea, warm, blue and misty. We splashed in the sea, swam a bit, Ness and Adam snogged on a towel under a beach umbrella till Dad made us all, even Mum and Gran, join in one of his football games with a beach ball and towels for goal posts. All our troubles seemed so far away etc. even Clarry had shut up. If I lived here with Gran, she'd go away for ever, I thought.

At last, worn out, we flopped down. I put on fresh sun lotion and listened to my favourite group. Dad said he'd walk Bowie a bit – you can't let him run loose on the beach.

'Dad's going to get a drink,' I said to Mum. 'That's his walk.'

'He deserves one,' she said.

'Why don't you go with him? I'll be with Troy. And Gran'll be with me, won't you, Gran?'

"Course, dear. Off you both go.'

And Mum and Dad went together, laughing a bit, lovely. It made me feel happy. Troy was drawing a kind of geometric shape in the sand with a stick, good as gold, Gran said, relax, relax, girl. Bliss. Then I fell asleep.

A maniac silhouetted black against the blazing sun was raving.

'If your xxxxxxx kid doesn't stop kicking sand all over us I'll tear him limb from limb. Stop him, stop him,' he shouted.

Not road rage, Troy rage, said Clarry in my head as I woke up.

I looked for Dad and Mum but there was only Gran and me. Adam and Ness had wandered off somewhere. Troy stood in the centre of what looked like a triangle with squares on each side holding a bucket and spade (a bucket and spade! what bucket and spade? hadn't got one earlier). He'd built several sand towers and was digging a moat round the whole lot.

The man was jumping up and down.

'Can't you see?' he roared at us. 'Your horrible little kid is kicking sand everywhere. He's blinded my wife and little Angeline's crying . . .'

'Sorry, I'm sorry . . .' I cried. Gran was still waking up and groping for her specs. 'Stop it, Troy.'

'I can't stop it. I'm building a twelve-sided fortress on the squares of my triangle with castles at each corner. It's beautiful. But I want more water in the moat to protect it from enemies.'

He waved his spade at the man. 'Enemies like him. Go away, nasty man.'

Gran stood up. All of five foot she is. For the first time ever I wished I'd got a big, fat Gran.

'Stop throwing sand everywhere, Troy. Say you're sorry.'

'More water! The moat needs more scooping out and more water!'

Sand flew everywhere, but mainly over a little girl aged about four who'd joined her Dad, howling. A woman who looked like the Revenge of the 50 Foot Woman in that old film came up behind her, rubbing her eyes, and a spotty teenager in a baseball cap and another smaller kid, shouting, 'He's took my bucket and spade.'

Best to run. Might get murdered, hissed Clarry, as the man shouted, 'We don't want your sort on the beach. Shove off! And take that horrible brat with you before I do something to 'im. Like killing 'im.'

'It's not your beach. I happen to live just over there,' Gran shouted back. 'Troy didn't mean to annoy you and he's sorry. Aren't you, Troy? Sorry? Troy?'

'No, I want to finish my fortress,' and Troy bent down to scoop up some more sand, sending it everywhere like a desert storm.

'Xxxx your fortress,' shouted the man and leapt on all the sandcastle towers, squashing them one by one. 'And if he's blinded my wife I'll sue you. I will!'

You'll spend years of your life being sued by people who hate Troy, muttered Clarry, down in my stomach. I was dead scared. The man was huge, his family frightening, just like the Addams Family. Gran was frightened, too. I could tell. She clutched my hand and reached out for Troy.

'Come on. Troy, let's go. Just let's go!'

But Troy stood rigid – his face a gold-and-brown tiger mask, his finger pointing at the man, eyes black slits of hatred and fury, little flat nose quivering with rage.

'YOU – WRECK – THINGS! YOU – WILL – DIE!'

Little Angeline howled and her father stepped forward, fists punching the air. I shut my eyes, waiting for the end.

And opened them.

'Are we all having fun?' laughed a voice. Ness stood there in her golden hair and her golden bikini and her golden bracelets and golden anklets, smiling and glistening in the sun. Tall, dark and tanned, Adam loomed behind her. Envy, jealousy had a battle with relief. Relief won.

She stooped down.

'Don't cry, little girl,' she beamed, 'you can have my ice-cream. It's lovely. Here. Taste.'

Little Angeline stopped crying and licked the ice-cream instead. The man dropped his fists. The woman and her boys stepped back. Troy stopped looking like Shere Khan out of *The Jungle Book*, picked up the bucket and spade and handed them over, scowling. Then he turned round and stalked off towards Gran's house. But Mum and Dad were coming towards us. Dad picked Troy up and threw him up into a fireman's lift. It's one of their games.

'I shan't never, never, never build a fortress again,' Troy gulped, upside down.

'You don't have to. There's no rule that you have to build a fortress,' Dad said, coming up to us. 'Let's go and eat instead.'

Chapter Five

1 Pick a number, e.g. 25
2 Write down age: 9
3 Double it: 18
4 Add five: 23
5 Multiply by hundred: 2300
6 Divide by two: 1150
7 Deduct number of days in year (365): 785
8 Add number first thought of (25): 810
9 Add 115: 925
10 Age is number on left 9; 25 on right is number first thought of.

Right up high on the cliff top the picnic Gran had fixed up earlier was spread out on the grass – chicken nuggets, fish fingers, sausages, sardines, French bread, salad, rolls, cheese, drinks and much, much more. Great! I stuffed and stuffed, but longed for forbidden chocolate. Ness won't touch it and Troy gets hyperactive and nutty (yeah, even more than usual). Dad was drinking a can of beer and so were Gran and Mum.

'A wonderful day,' Mum sighed. 'Best day we've had for ages.'

After Dad had arrived with Mum and Bowie the Addams Family had disappeared, vamoosed. Then we'd picked up all our gear and made our way up the paths and the steps to the cliff top, away from the crowds, to have our picnic and it was so peaceful up there lying on the grass looking out over the bay, the turquoise-blue and green-ultramarine sea, the misty magical faraway cliffs. I was in my fantasy world. It doesn't have Ness and Troy in it. Nor Clarry. *I'm* in control there.

Adam and Ness were sprawled out on a rug in a little world of their own; Gran was reading *Pride and Prejudice* for the hundredth time, Mum was scribbling away at one of her stories, Dad doing a crossword, Troy writing out numbers in his exercise book, me pretending to look at my notes on the Aztecs (test next week) but really reading a horror story tucked in my history file. I love horror stories: '. . . *the weeping heroine left her friends and followed a lonely, overgrown path leading into a dark primeval wood growing thicker and more scary till there before her stood an ancient, ruined tower with a wooden door, studded with rusty nails. A torn and dirty notice hangs there, "Enter At Your Peril". She pushed open the door and she entered. A moan from the dark at the back of the door, a cry from the hooded crow perched on the wooden stairway ahead of her in the gloom . . .*'

Aowh, whispered Clarry, joining in. *Don't go on. Yes, do go on. Read some more.* I did. Horror always seems so safe to me after home life with Troy.

'*Waltzing Matilda, Waltzing Matilda,*' the theme tune of Dad's mobile phone began to ring.

'Where the xxxx is the xxxxxxx thing?' he yelled, scrabbling through all our gear to find it.

'In the pocket of your shirt. Over there! There! What did you have to bring it for? It was perfect without it!'

'OK. I'm not answering it.'

At last the phone stopped ringing. Soon we were all quiet again until Gran fell asleep and snorted in her snooze.

'What's "mad man on the moon" in seven letters?'

'Lunatic,' said Mum.

'Troy,' said Ness, looking up. '. . . oh, no, it's only four letters.'

Troy looked up and glared.

'Leave him alone. Don't stir things, Ness,' Gran said, waking up.

We settled down again, sleepy after all the food. *Go on reading*, Clarry said.

'*Waltzing Matilda, Waltzing Matilda*,' rang Dad's mobile again. He and Mum looked at one another.

'You'd better answer it. There might be a fire at the office or our house might have fallen down,' Mum said.

'I wish it would. I hate my job, and home is like living in a goldfish bowl. I want to live where there's room to breathe and there's no neighbours to tell us what Troy's done next and their advice on what we ought to do about him. I want room to be ME! Somewhere like this!' He waved his hand at the sea and woods and hills in the fading distance.

Mum pulled a face.

'Not sure I want you being YOU! Might be a bit much. Just answer the phone.'

'I wish someone would get rid of it. I hate phones, mobiles, the lot,' Dad reached for his shirt. But Troy had already got there.

'If you don't want it, Dad, I'll throw it away for you.

I'll throw the nasty noisy thing over the cliff! One – two – three!'

'No! No! Don't! Troy! Don't!' The words hung in the air. I could almost see balloons round them. How many times had the Spiers family yelled those words? Tens? Hundreds? Thousands? Just . . . too many . . .

. . . as Troy threw the mobile in the shirt pocket over the edge of the cliff.

There was a silence lasting a century. Probably only a couple of seconds. Eternity to us. Ever and ever and ever. And then from down below us came a terrible cry.

'There's a beach down there,' whispered Adam, who'd wriggled on his stomach to the awful edge and peered over. I hid my eyes. Clarry and me, we're only brave in stories.

'I think the mobile's hit somebody. There's someone jumping up and shouting and another lying flat out,' Adam reported.

'Let's run,' Vanessa said. 'Let's get away quickly. It's probably bashed his head in falling from that height and I don't want to go to prison for murder. It isn't exactly the latest model, and it's heavy.'

She pulled the towel round her and started to head for the far-away hills.

'No, we have to go down,' Dad's voice was a hundred years old. 'It's OK – you lot all go. Back to Gran's. It's my mobile. I'll say I dropped it accidentally. Stop crying, Claire. Crying doesn't sort things out.'

'It's just that everything always goes wrong for us when I want it to be perfect.' I sobbed. 'Something always spoils things.'

'Not something. *Him*!' Ness said, looking round and jerking a thumb at Troy.

'Me? Why? I didn't do anything. Dad wanted someone to get rid of his mobile so I did. I didn't like it either. The numbers were put on in a nasty way.'

Mum said, 'Let's do what Jack says. He'll deal with it.' She started to gather up our stuff.

Gran shook her head. 'That's not fair. If someone's really hurt there'll be a lot of trouble and Jack will cop it. They'll be more lenient with Troy. And he must start to face up to the trouble he causes.'

'What trouble? What trouble do I cause?'

The shouts were near and loud and hostile. The man had nearly arrived at the top. Ness came back to us. Adam held her hand, Gran held Troy's and Dad held Mum's as we all drew together to meet – what? I'd only got Clarry so I wrapped my arms round my tum where she often seems to be.

And so we waited at the cliff top for the man to reach us.

The man wasn't dead. There wasn't a body splattered all over the beach, squashed by Dad's falling mobile. He was there in front of us with the other one who'd been standing and shouting at us. Next, a woman arrived panting up the cliff steps after them. They were angry and agitated and puffed and red-faced because it's steep, that climb up from the beach. We were all saying sorry, over and over again and smiling like crazy, but not Troy who was gazing at the blue sky and counting seagulls, I think. I quietly gave him a kick, but he moved away as if none of this silly fuss was anything to do with him and not in the least interesting. Apologizing to people you've nearly flattened is boring. That's Troy.

But all our sorries didn't help.

The nearly splattered man, wearing red shorts, had red hair and was red all over, from sunburn and rage, I think. He was absolutely terrifying. He held the mobile in his hand and yelled, 'You know what I'm gonna do with this!'

'Don't do it,' interrupted Gran. 'You're very hot and red – you look as if you might have a heart attack. Take care – be careful. None of this is worth it – it was all an accident. And we're very sorry.'

'That lunatic –' pointing at Dad – 'nearly killed me. He's a menace. He shouldn't be allowed out . . .'

'Not among decent, peaceful people,' squeaked the woman.

'And so I'm gonna do to you what you did to me!'

He hurled the mobile at Dad, who ducked while the mobile flew through the air and smashed, slap, bang, wallop, into a man walking along with his arm round a very pretty girl. A scream of rage and pain and shrieks of shock, horror, rang out over the cliffs and flew out over the blue, blue sea mingling with cries of surprise and terror from everyone really, except Troy. The roaring of the red man changed to 'Oh, my Lord,' when he realized that it wasn't Dad he'd hit.

A strange moment's silence fell on us like a cloud

except for Ness saying, 'That's a very mobile mobile.'

That stuck in my head but it was days before that I got the message.

Clarry was chanting, *Run, run, as fast as you can*, like an old nursery rhyme – so I got out of the way as both lots turned on Dad, who like me was heading for the cliff stairs when a whistle blew – shrill and sharp, cutting through everything.

Gran stood there – blowing on the whistle she always carries in case she's attacked and . . . 'Just you behave yourselves!!' she called, exactly like years ago when she was a schoolteacher – so everyone eased down, looking a bit silly and the whistle screech died away and Bowie growled menacingly, patrolling all round us, fur-hackled, brave, lovely Bowie.

'We're sorry,' announced Dad. 'And we're leaving now. Goodbye. Let me wish you all a very happy holiday here from all of us. Goodbye now.'

Backing away from everyone, Dad waving like the Queen and smiling like a makeover presenter with a bare chest, we headed for the steps and began to descend, getting faster and faster as we went. As we scrambled down one after another I could hear Dad muttering, 'Troy! Gorblimey, why do you do this to us? What have we done to deserve you? Surely I haven't been that wicked? I'm not a saint, I know, but getting you? Is there no justice? No mercy? We've made enemies of nearly everybody on the beach!'

'Self-pity,' answered Gran, 'never got anyone anywhere. Troy is a fine boy, really. Aren't you, Troy?'

'I dunno what you're talking about, Gran. And what were those people shouting for? I was busy working out what was the highest primary number I could get to in my head. Those silly people were a nuisance 'cos they put me off and I shall have to start again.'

Dad was carrying brave Bowie, who's an awful coward about heights, over steep steps. We all landed in a heap at the bottom of the cliff, nearly falling over each other. Then Mum said,

'Jack, you've left your mobile up there, haven't you?'

'If you think I'm going back up there to get it you've got another thing coming. It's probably smashed to bits by now and anyway it's time I got a new one, I suppose. But I hate the wretched things. C'mon, let's get back to Gran's. I don't want to hang about.'

Ness said later she saw faces looking over from the cliff top, but I was too scared and too busy hurrying to look up.

We said goodbye to Gran and went back home. All was friendly back in Thorneycroft Crescent. People were speaking to us again. Matthew Taylor, said Vanessa, had taken to watching her with field glasses out of his attic window and there was news about Mr Fortescue-Corbett. He'd swapped his Merc for a Porsche and had taken to wearing jeans and T-shirts and trainers. His wife had left him apparently, and gone home to her mother. He could often be seen jogging down one side of Thorneycroft Crescent and back round the other past our house.

Next he took to smiling and saying, 'Hello, little fellow,' to Troy. That was a waste of time. Troy spat or scowled back but Mr F-Corbett just went on smiling.

He's got a crush on Vanessa, Clarry told me.

'Don't be crazy. He's ancient.'

No, not really, only forty or so. He'll be talking to her soon. You'll see.

'No way! Besides, she loves Adam.'

Then Adam had to go to London for a university interview. He was staying there with his sister for a few days.

'Giles has asked me out for dinner,' Vanessa said to the mirror in her bedroom as she attacked a spot on the end of her nose. She was mad with it, the spot, I mean.

'Giles? Who's he when he's at home?' I asked.

'Giles? Oh, Giles Fortescue-Corbett.'

'Nah . . . You're having me on. Are you going?'

'Yes. I don't see why not if Adam's clubbing up in London and I bet he does, when he's finished his interviews. But don't tell Mum or Dad – they wouldn't approve.'

'But . . . *Him*! He's *antique*.'

'No, he's not. You're just a baby and don't understand. Giles is quite dishy. And seriously rich, you know, little Claire. Loaded.'

'Claire!' Mum yelled. 'Go and find Troy.'

'Oh, OK. Can't Troy look after himself, Mum?'

I wanted to hear more of Ness's ideas on older men.

'No! Go and find him.'

I knew he'd be in the green island in the middle of all

the thorn bushes. With Bowie. I thought I'd go and join him 'cos I don't understand anything – though I'M NOT JUST A BABY, like Vanessa says. Giles, Mr Fortescue-Bender – I mean Corbett – he's horrible.

But safe in the little island I was licked by Bowie and Troy smiled at me. He has a wonderful smile when you get to see it. About once a year. Maybe he's OK. I mean, all boys are horrible, aren't they? Perhaps he's normal really. I do love him even when he drives me crazy. When he smiles like that, anyway. Clarry, shut up.

Chapter Six

Number Two, Number Two
They all like me and some like you.

I've been on lots of sleepovers at my friends' houses, but when it came to me having one, Mum always chickened out. But surprise, surprise, Dad said when I asked again that he didn't see why not, there was no reason why Troy should come first all the time and when I'd picked myself off the floor (where I'd fallen down with shock) I got around to asking my friends, Kim, of course, Beth, Lily and Abby, yes, they could all come, great and Ness would baby-sit (ha, ha) providing the about-to-return and dishy, pop-idol, lovely Adam could come.

'No need,' Mum said. 'I shan't go out.'

'Oh, yes, you will,' spoke Dad. 'You and I will have an evening out. Like other people do. Vanessa will baby-sit. She's almost eighteen and Troy is out of nappies. Or hadn't you noticed?'

'Oh, all right, I suppose. But I shall worry.'

'Oh, for heaven's sake. You can ring up every hour on the hour. Like you did last time we dared to poke our noses out of this sacred dwelling. Better still, just remember, Ness, to ring us every five minutes. Just text "Troy OK", "House OK", "Dog OK", and so on.'

'Don't go on. I've got your message,' said Mum.

'Good. And talk to me like you used to. Before the Trojan Age.'

'Trojan Age? What are you on about?'

'Trojan Age. You know there was a golden, hap- hap-happy time before we had him and everything went crazy.'

'You are *so* unfair. He'll be fine. He's nice looking . . .'

'Yeah, I know – everyone tells us so. What I want to hear is how *nicely* he behaves. Instead of he's weird, he's crazy, he's lost his marbles!'

'It's you that's crazy, saying all these horrible things – what chance has he got with you for a father, I'd like to know?'

'SHUT UP! SHUT UP! Both of you!' I yelled. 'You don't want him to hear you, do you? I'm sick of your rows.'

'Don't you speak to me like that, Claire, or you can cancel the sleepover.'

Tears came into my eyes. It was so unfair. Mum was always unfair to me, but then, 'Don't cry,' she said. 'It's OK. We'll go out and Vanessa and Adam will stay in. You look a bit peaky anyway. Stop worrying. What's the matter?'

'Nothing.'

The doorbell rang. Adam had arrived, back from London.

'Who are you? What are you doing here? It's not your house,' Troy said.

'Take no notice of him. He's bonkers,' cried Ness.

'Don't you remember me, then, Troy?' asked Adam.

'Never seen you before.'

'It's OK, Adam,' said Dad. 'Take no notice. It's just him. It's what we live with. But his mother insists he's normal.'

Mum slammed out of his room, but not before I saw a tear roll down her face.

'Oh, it's you, Adam,' said Troy. 'You don't want to go snogging with that girl. She's my sister and she's boring. Come and play with me.'

And Troy dragged Adam off to one of his games. Adam played for a while till Ness came out with: 'If you don't stop playing that stupid game, we're finished!'

'OK, OK, Vanessa. Sorry, Troy. I've got to go.'

Troy grabbed him by the legs, but Adam got away.

My sleepover was fixed up OK. I got my room tidied up for the great occasion and even gave it a new coat of lilac-coloured paint to impress my friends who were all going to sleep in there. First time. Bit messy, but OK.

Mum and Dad went out after she'd checked everything three times and made Ness promise she'd stay in.

'Even if there's an earthquake and the house falls down you – must – not – leave – the – house!' Dad mouthed at Ness.

'Well, I wouldn't, would I? I'd be lying under the rubble. Dead probably.'

'Don't say such things!' Mum cried.

'Come on, Julie. Let's go.'

They went off, niggly and cross, but I forgot as my friends poured inside, Kim singing, Abby, Lily, Beth.

46

My friends. Mine. The hall filled up with sleeping bags, videos, books, bags stuffed with pyjamas and whatever, make-up, food, sweets, everything. Suddenly the world was great, the sun shining through the stained-glass window in the hall colouring everything like a rainbow and we were the pot of gold at the end of it, Bowie barking and jumping, then Ness and Adam laughing at us.

'He's dishy. Wow!' Kim said, as they settled somewhere else.

'But Ness is gorgeous too, isn't she?'

'She's OK. She'll do.'

What a wonderful world. Clarry was keeping quiet. Kim was here. Clarry usually keeps quiet when Kim's around. We put on music and started to sort out things in the living room, Bowie helping and jumping on everything. Someone had given Lily a nail-varnish kit with cool frosted colours, pink, blue, green, golden, silver, red, purple, lilac, turquoise, ultramarine, shinier, glimmer, magic, all the colours of the universe and we stood them on the mantelpiece, shining there. Everything was coming up rainbow jacketed.

Except for a black cloud that appeared in the doorway.

'How can I do anything with you lot around? I can't play a game. I can't do my project. You're all horrible! Go away! Go away!' he was screaming. 'I shall kill you all!'

'Oh, come on, Troy. You know us. You know me.' That was Kim. 'We'll play with you as well. We won't mess up any of your things. Come on, Troy. We're your friends.'

'I don't have friends. I don't want friends. I just want you all to go away. Or you can die.'

'Please don't be like that. We like you, Troy. We do. You've got a big room upstairs. We'll carry your stuff up there and we won't disturb you. Honest?'

'Well – yes. But don't mess up anything of mine, will you? Promise? Kim?'

Kim grinned at me. 'He knows me. I've got through. OK, Troy. You go on up. We'll leave you alone.'

'I shall want my beans. In an opened can. With a spoon.'

That's how he eats. He hates eating with anyone else. Except Bowie.

'I'll do that, Troy,' I said.

He almost smiled and went upstairs. I took him his can of beans and we could hear him singing his number songs. And we began singing our songs and playing our games, Twister, card games, PlayStation etc. Everything hip-hop, wow! Next we wanted to have a go at Junior Trivial Pursuit, but found we hadn't got any dice. I knew that Troy had some. Kim said she'd ask him because I didn't want to since I was pretty sure he wouldn't want to.

Kim came down holding the dice and grinning happily.

'He's fallen asleep in the middle of writing out a lot of numbers on a long piece of paper going all round his room. He looked sweet!'

Clarry came into my head at last to wonder how sweet he'd look when he found out we'd taken his dice, but I shut her up, telling her that he'd probably finished playing now. We played Trivial Pursuit for a while, finished off our grub, then went into the front room and watched a really spooky horror video, which took our minds off everything else, including Troy.

By the time it had finished it had gone past midnight. Mum and Dad still hadn't got back from their night out and Vanessa and Adam were nowhere to be seen. Bet they've slipped out somewhere. Or gone to bed. Speaking of bed . . .

'Do you want to go up now?' I suggested, feeling quite tired after that film.

Everyone agreed and we all trooped upstairs to find . . . to find . . . to find . . . my newly painted bedroom covered in numbers painted from . . . the pretty nail varnish bottles. Troy had taken them off the mantelpiece and used them on my room. My newly decorated room. I somehow wasn't surprised. *You'd known all along*, Clarry said in my head.

My friends all stood there in shock. I sagged down on the bed. The numbers were everywhere, everywhere he could get to. If he could've reached the ceiling it would've been numbered as well.

'It looks like a new kind of art,' said Lily.

'Graffiti, more like,' said Abby.

'It's not funny,' I said. 'Mum and Dad'll do their nut when they see it.'

'Just tell your mum Troy did it. It's not your fault,' said Beth.

'Mum never blames him for anything. It's 'cos we used his dice. That's why he did this.'

'Let's try and rub it off before they come back,' suggested Kim.

We all went to the bathroom and grabbed wet flannels. I poked my nose in at Troy. He was asleep in his bed by now. I nearly woke him up to make him help. But why bother? He'd only be a nuisance.

'I'll murder you, I will, one day! Once, just once, let me have fun!'

We all rubbed and scrubbed away at the walls, but it wasn't any good. It wouldn't come off.

'I've got another idea,' said Kim, always full of ideas, like a cat full of fleas. 'Have you got any of that paint left, Claire?'

'Yep. I've only used about half of it.'

'Well, then, let's all start painting over the numbers.'

'We won't have time before Mum and Dad get back. And when they see this they won't let me have another sleepover. And it was great! I hate my brother!'

'When they come in we'll turn the light off and pretend to be asleep. They might not come in the room then.'

'Let's do it,' said Beth. 'It'll be a laugh.'

So we went and got the paint, rollers, brushes and newspapers to cover the floor and we all got stuck in, painting over the numbers. We kept giggling and it wasn't the best paint job ever. Then about half an hour later, just past one o'clock, we heard the front door open.

'Lights out,' said Kim. 'They're back.'

So we shoved everything into my wardrobe and crawled into our sleeping bags.

'The house is still standing.' I could hear Dad in the hall. 'Amazing.'

'Everyone must have gone to bed,' said Mum, pushing Bowie off. He was the only one there to greet them.

'That's where I'm heading in a minute as well,' said Dad. I heard him open the front room door where we'd been watching the video. 'Everything seems quite tidy. I don't believe it.'

They rustled about a bit down below, then we heard footsteps coming up the stairs. We snuggled down in our sleeping bags, trying not to giggle.

'Look, Troy's fallen asleep with his light on,' said Mum, going in and turning it off. 'He's sweet! Shall I look in on the girls?'

'No, I don't think so. Not if they're asleep. You'll disturb them. Let sleeping dogs lie!'

'I just want to see if they're all right.'

'They'll be fine, Julie. Don't fuss.'

Just before they reached their bedroom they went past Vanessa's, who wasn't there.

'I see they went out after all,' said Dad. 'Some baby-sitters they are.'

'Well, everything seems to be OK. Troy doesn't seem to have done anything.'

'That'll be a first, then.'

We heard their bedroom door shut, gave them a few minutes to settle down, then turned the light back on and started painting again.

'We'll get this done before morning,' said Kim. 'Then your Mum and Dad won't even know anything happened.'

'I hope not,' I said.

There was one close shave when Dad woke up to go to the bathroom in the middle of the night, but apart from that, no problems. We finished at about four in the morning, tiptoed to the bathroom to wash any paint off us, then went and slept the sleep of the just.

Next morning at about ten o'clock my bedroom door opened and Mum peered in. We were still all lying flat out.

'You must have had a late night like us,' she smiled. 'Would you like me to make you some breakfast?'

'Yes, please,' we all said.

'You're OK, Claire,' whispered Kim. 'She hasn't noticed anything.'

'Great. So we might be able to do this again. She won't have any reason to say No.'

We all went downstairs in high spirits and scoffed the breakfast down, chatting about what we were going to do with the day. Troy was there and I gave him a look which didn't bother him. He'd probably forgotten all about it by now, thinking up a new football game or something.

Then I remembered I'd left my purse upstairs and went up to get it. On the way I met Dad and he held up his hand. What was he doing that for? Then I looked more closely and saw that it was covered in paint.

'I went in to draw your curtains and turn the light off. You must have used some very slow-drying paint when you did your room.' He grinned. 'It doesn't normally take three days to dry in my experience.'

I rushed past him, not wanting to explain and joined
my friends downstairs.

'Let's go out! Quick!'

'Why? What's the rush?'

'Dad's sussed out the paint.'

'How?'

'He put his hand in it.'

'Oh, right.'

So we all nipped out while Dad washed his hands off
in the bathroom. But he never said anything, though he
knew something was up. He's OK, my dad.

Chapter Seven

		Troy		Dad		Mum
Year born		1992		1960		1964
Year started	School	1997	Work	1978	Married	1984
Age at end of year		11		43		39
Number of years since starting	School	6	Work	25	Married	19
TOTAL		4006		4006		4006

Answer is always double the current year.
Halve 4006 to get the current year – 2003.

Clarry was grumbling and muttering in my head, telling me what to do as usual. But I didn't want to do what she was saying. I don't talk about school at home. It's dangerous. It's embarrassing. It's boring. *But you ought to warn her, Claire,* went on Clarry. *It's only fair. And it's not about you. It's about HIM.* So when, at last, when me and Mum were on our own:

'We're having sex education at school, Mum,' I said.

'Good,' she smiled. 'It won't bother you and your crowd, will it? You all seem so clued about everything.'

'You think it's a good idea, then?'

'Oh, yes. Very sensible. And it's not new. They gave sex lessons when I was at school. Old Mr Cantellow gave ours. He was a nice old boy. We made little models in Plasticine – we used Plasticine – with lids on the Mum's tum that you lifted up to see the baby inside. I got a gold star for mine. And I remember . . .'

'MUM!' I had to stop her. She'll go on for ever about *her* school days.

'Yes, Claire, it's OK. Your father and I don't mind. I know some parents object but we don't. And if there's anything you don't understand just ask me. Or Vanessa. She probably knows more about it than I do. Kids these days . . .'

'MUM!'

'Just don't worry about . . .'

'MUM! Shut up and LISTEN! It's not me that's the problem. It's Troy.'

'Is he having sex education as well?'

'Yeah. All his year. As well as ours.'

'OH!'

'Yeah. That's a bit different, isn't it?'

'It is a bit. Fancy that! Troy and sex education!'

And she burst out laughing. She laughed and laughed, face red, tears rolling down her cheeks.

'Bet he numbers all the bits and pieces,' she cried.

I was shocked. 'MUM!'

She wouldn't stop laughing. Was she going to have hysterics?

'I thought you'd take it seriously,' I cried, fetching her a glass of water.

'I am. I am,' she spluttered, still laughing.

After a minute she calmed down.

'Thanks for telling me, Claire. I'll be on the lookout. And I'll tell Jack. I think we shouldn't say anything to Troy and it will all pass over without any problems. I wonder if he'll mention it to us?'

She told Dad that evening 'cos I heard them talking and laughing together. I thought they were horrible – but then parents often are. They don't listen. They don't think you have feelings. Mine were only interested in Troy. 'Claire's a good girl. She'll do it OK,' they say. They don't *know* me.

That's why they're an endangered species, Clarry said when I looked in the mirror and checked my brace that night.

'What d'you mean?'

How many in your class have got both *parents living together, I mean – not living with someone else?*

'Not many. Less than half. We're lucky. I wonder why?'

You see. Parents are dying out.

'I don't like that. Mum and Dad *must* stay together.'

Oh. Give me a reason.

'Mum and me couldn't manage Troy on our own. Suppose he had one of his tantrums. Besides . . .'

Besides what?

'I don't want them to split! I love them. And I love Dad. He's funny. He makes me laugh. I hope Troy doesn't drive him away. He does love Troy, doesn't he?'

Sure. You all love Troy.

'I suppose so. I don't like this conversation. It's embarrassing. Shut up, Clarry. I'm going to bed.'

Dad stood on the landing still laughing.

'I'll wait and see what he makes of it,' he roared.

* * *

'We needn't have worried. Come and look. Don't disturb him,' whispered Mum.

'It'd take an earthquake to disturb him when he's playing a game,' said Dad.

Troy had placed his football team on his green square. He does it very carefully and goes ballistic if he's disturbed. He was concentrating hard, but he wasn't using his Premiership Teams or even the City Schools Football League names as he usually does.

'Listen,' whispered Dad.

Loudly Troy announced his game's final score.

'Testicles 6 – Nipples United 2.'

He jumped up and down clapping loudly,

'And Testicles are the Champions!!! Hooray! They're Top of the League!'

Back in the kitchen,

'We needn't have worried,' Mum smiled. 'Troy has got it all sorted.'

'Yes, sex is a football game,' Dad grinned. 'Funny. I never thought of it like that.'

But next day was one of those days, doomed from dawn to dusk. Rain poured down like sharp, wet needles. I couldn't find my homework and Troy wouldn't be shifted from his testicles and nipples game. So I was late for school and got told off and then in the lunch hour I fell down and grazed my knee badly. Molly Haynes and some other cretins laughed at me as I limped round the corner with Kim to get it sorted and there we saw Troy standing face to the wall with Mrs Kittigrew, my least favourite dinner lady, waggling her finger like a poison thistle as she told him off. I could tell from the way he was standing he'd have his tiger-tiger look on. Oh, no, not trouble again.

'What's he done?' I asked Mrs Kittigrew.

'None of your business!' Then she spotted my knee. 'You'd better get that tended to, instead of fussing about your brother who's a very naughty boy. Go along now.'

Kim said, 'Please tell us what Troy's done.'

'Spitting. Spitting all over some children. We can't have that sort of thing, can we? I didn't know anyone had got that much spit in them. Disgusting. He ought to be brought up better. I'm surprised your mother allows it, Claire.'

'But why was he spitting?' Kim's very persistent. My knee was hurting horribly. I wanted to go. But I worried about Troy.

'No reason. Perfectly nice boys.'

'No, they're not very nice boys,' said the face turned to the wall. 'They're very nasty. I shall kill them.'

'You see!' shouted Mrs Kittigrew. 'What a naughty boy! You mustn't talk like that. And you mustn't spit.'

'What did they do to you?' Kim spoke straight to Troy.

My knee was stabbing and throbbing now. *Leave it, Kim*, Clarry kept saying. *Let's look after Claire. Somebody look after Claire for once.*

'They wanted me to play *their* game and I wanted to play my football game with the dice and write it in my book. They threw my book and dice over the school railings into the road and a little kid ran off with them. So I shouted and spat. And *she*,' he swung round from the wall and looked at us, 'came along and made me stand here and I'm going to get reported.'

His brown eyes slitted, dark, angry and sad. He flicked back his streaky yellow hair – yes, the tiger look was there.

I forgot my leg.

'But that's not fair, Mrs Kittigrew, they took his book. He loves his book.'

'Well, he didn't tell me. He just stood there spitting and saying swear words. Very wrong. Why didn't you tell me and I could have got you your book back?'

'I thought you were too stupid,' said Troy.

That did it. Back he was turned to the wall to be reported later. I was sent inside to get my knee sorted out.

It hurt and I cried a bit, though some of it was for Troy. I know how much his book meant. And I knew *he* wouldn't cry. He doesn't. Tigers don't, do they?

The day hasn't finished playing nasties with us, Clarry said. Mum was too harassed when we got home to listen to us, just saying, 'Troy, you mustn't ever spit,' and then, 'Will you tidy up, Claire, and get the best plates and things out and see they're clean?'

'What for? Mum, my leg hurts!'

'Never mind, dear. It'll soon be better. Now see if we've got those wine glasses Gran gave us – the ones Dad won't use – get them out and check them.'

'MUM!'

'Oh, please help me, Claire!'

'What are you flapping about? And listen, will you? We've both had a horrible time at school and you don't care, do you? Why all the fuss?'

'Your Dad's bringing home a man who might have an interesting job for him, one he'll like. And he's bringing his wife . . .'

'Wife?'

'Well, partner, I don't know. And I said I'd do a meal. I don't know why. I must be crazy 'cos you know, Claire, I'm a rotten cook.'

'MUM. We don't do that sort of thing. We eat our own things. Remember. We don't sit down all proper! Except at Christmas.'

'Get out of the way – I want to spread my game out on the floor,' said Troy. 'And I need a new book for my projects.'

'No, not tonight, Troy.'

He took no notice and started to spread his green baize cloth on the floor. Mum began pulling it up. She was really agitated now. Mum does get agitated. She always throws a wobbly if there's cooking to do and if there are GUESTS coming.

'Troy! Troy! Oh, Vanessa, there you are! Give me a hand. Your father's got someone coming and I want to tidy the place up and get a meal ready.'

'Well, I want to go out.'

'Oh, no! I thought you'd stay in, make yourself look nice and play the piano for us.'

Ness is doing Music A-levels, plays like an angel. Just one more reason why she thinks she's the bee's knees.

Mum would like her to show off occasionally, but Vanessa does what *she* wants, not what Mum would like.

'No way! Jane Austen's dead! Haven't you heard? We don't sit listening to the heroine play her five easy pieces any more. Now, Mum. Don't bother to clear up. He'll either like Dad or he won't. We won't matter tuppence to him. Send out for a takeaway. And Troy, move. Play that in your room.'

Troy looked up, glared, but got his stuff and went upstairs. Sometimes he wins, sometimes Ness. Whatever.

Mum collapsed on a chair.

'Yeah. Sorry. I'm an idiot. Just stress. Let's be comfortable. Of course I don't have to cook a six-course meal. Now, Claire, what's the matter with your knee? And what's all this about Troy spitting and losing his book?'

I told her about all of it and she found another book for him.

He left his game to come down and collect it.

'Thanks,' he muttered, 'but it isn't the same as my real book.' He was blinking hard, but not crying.

She didn't take much interest in my knee though it was badly grazed and hurting a lot.

'I'll go to school and see that dinner lady. I'm not having her bullying Troy.'

You see, Clarry whispered to me. *It's always Troy. You don't matter. He's her BOY!*

Dad's guests seemed to like Dad and Mum. I didn't take much notice because my knee hurt and I felt rotten. But

Dad was laughing and Mum was pink and pretty so I guessed everything was OK.

'We haven't seen your boy,' said Ted Portman, or whatever his name was. I didn't like him much. Wibbly tash. Wobbly chins. She, Tamsin or Tansy, was pretty, but not as pretty as Ness. After a while, he said, 'We've heard a lot about your boy. Where is he? Have you put him to bed?'

Troy'd gone up with an open can of baked beans and a spoon. Like I said, he won't eat with strangers at all, so Mum lets him eat what he wants.

'No. Troy puts himself to bed.'

'Must be quite a character, ho, ho, ho. We'd love to see him. Call him down.'

Mum wasn't looking so good now. Not so pink and pretty.

'He doesn't like to be disturbed.'

'Oh, I say! Who's he? The Queen?'

'He's a bit awkward.'

'I think you spoil him. Kids need discipline. I wouldn't let him behave like that, and it's not like you, Jack.' My dad just grinned. 'Go on, bring him downstairs.'

'I'll get him,' said Ness, ending this awful conversation.

Troy stood in the doorway.

'Why, he's really nice!' cried Tamsin or Tansy. 'You didn't tell us how good-looking he is. Come and say hello, little boy.'

Of course Troy didn't say hello. He stared at her as if she was something under a microscope. It was a wonder he didn't make one of his sick noises. 'I want to finish my game,' he said.

Ness was grinning her head off, but I hid mine. I couldn't bear this. I got up to go, remembering to ask to be excused, Claire Creep being my name.

'What have you been doing at school, then?' Tamsin or Tansy went on. 'Anything nice?'

'Sex education.'

'Oh, was it interesting?' they giggled.

'Very peculiar. Do you two make babies like that? You must be seriously weird,' said Troy.

I didn't hear any more. I was out of the room and going up the stairs as fast as my hurt leg would let me go.

Chapter Eight

Troy's Dice Football Game

Any teams – International, Premiership, League, School etc.
One dice or two.

Home Team: ⚀ = I goal, ⚁ = 2 goals, ⚂ = 3 goals, ⚃ = 4 goals,
⚄ = 5 goals, ⚅ = no goals.

Away Team: ⚀ = I goal, ⚁ = 2 goals, ⚂ = 3 goals, ⚃ = 4 goals,
⚄ = no goals, ⚅ = no goals.

Dad seemed to be in a cheery mood over the last week or so, which was a relief for the rest of us – not to have him moaning and grumbling round the place.

'I'm glad you're happy again,' said Mum. 'You've been a bit like a bear with a sore head since you didn't get that Portman job.'

'I'm not bothered now because I think I'm up for promotion soon. Sales have gone up and I'm going to bring them the good news at the next board meeting which is tomorrow. I've been writing up what I'm going to say.'

'And nobody has complained about Troy for a few days either,' said Mum. 'Things must be looking up. Perhaps our luck has changed.'

'Yes, he's been very quiet – especially for a half-term holiday. They're usually hell when he's at home.'

I wouldn't bet on your luck changing, my other self, Clarry, whispered as I listened from the top of the stairs.

'Shut up,' I muttered back. 'I know why Troy hasn't been bothering anyone recently. He's busy with a new project.'

Troy had got hold of a fixture book for the whole of the season's football matches and had been playing his dice football game with it and working out the league tables for all the teams using up stacks of paper. As fast as he used it up he needed more. No one minded. Anything to keep Troy happy.

Next morning, however, the house was back to its usual chaos, Dad rushing about getting ready for his big day and Troy yelling the place down because some of his bits of paper were missing.

'What's happened to my scores? Where are they? I need them!'

'Where you left them,' replied Ness.

This bit of unhelpful information didn't do a lot for Troy, who started bellowing even louder.

'Well, I'm all ready to go,' said Dad holding his brief-case under his arm. 'Wish me luck. I'll leave you to Troy.'

'Thanks,' I muttered under my breath.

'Shut up, Troy,' Mum shouted up the stairs. 'Stop making a fuss about nothing.'

'It's not nothing. I'm halfway through the season now and if I can't find those bits of paper I'll have to start all over again.'

'Well, just look for them instead of yelling, then.'

'I have. They're not in my room. I've looked everywhere in there.'

'They must be somewhere else, then.'

'Perhaps they've been chucked away,' I suggested. 'In the dustbins.'

'The dustbins!!' Awful language followed. I hoped Ma Haynes wasn't listening. 'I'll go and turn them out!'

'No, you won't. I will,' gasped Mum. 'I don't want litter thrown all over the road and the garden, thank you. Claire, you search the rest of the house. Please.'

'Yes, Mum,' I sighed. Nothing is more boring than searching for someone else's stuff.

'I don't suppose you'll lend a hand?' I asked Ness.

'Can't. Too busy,' she replied, sprawled out on the carpet reading a magazine.

I left her to it, searched the living room, tried the kitchen, the front room and then Dad's study. Why can't Troy do his numbers on Dad's computer, I thought? I wouldn't be looking for his bits of paper, then. But Dad banned any of us going on it without his permission and Troy was banned full stop. Then I spotted something.

'Mum,' I called out.

'What?' a voice came from outside where Mum was looking through the dustbins. 'You've found them, I hope. These bins are disgusting.'

'No, I've found something else. Come and look.'

'What is it?'

'I think I've found Dad's notes on the talk he's giving for his meeting.'

Mum rushed in and looked over the sheet of paper

with Corals Computers, the company name, written on the top.

'Oh, no, I think you're right. He read it out to me last night. It's the same one.'

'He hasn't forgotten it, has he?'

'No, I don't think so. He was packing his briefcase very carefully last night.'

'P'raps he made another copy, then.'

'I'm not sure. He never mentioned it if he did.'

Doom, doom, wait for it, Clarry was whispering.

'I think I saw Troy writing some of his numbers down on this headed paper yesterday. He said he'd run out again.'

'You don't think Dad's taken Troy's numbers by mistake, do you?' gasped Mum.

'Yes. That's why we can't find Troy's numbers and Dad's speech is here.'

'TROY!' we both yelled.

'What? You found my numbers yet?' came a voice from the bedroom.

'No. Have you been using Dad's paper?'

'Yeah. Why?'

Me and Mum looked at each other.

'What are we gonna do?' I asked.

'Get after him, of course. With his notes. The meeting might not have started yet. He hasn't been gone very long.'

'Do you know where to go?'

'Yes. Corals Computers is on the Industrial Estate. I've been there a few times.'

'Do you want me to come with you?'

'If you want to. What about Troy, though?'

'Ness is here. She can look after him. She's staying put at the moment – working hard, she says.'

'All right. We'd better get moving. Ness, we're going out,' called Mum. 'Can you stay with Troy while we're gone?'

'If you want,' came the reply.

'If it's not too much trouble for you,' I added.

'Where are you going?' came Troy's voice.

'To get your numbers back and try and save Dad's skin at the same time.'

We ran out of the house and jumped into Mum's old banger.

Naturally we got stuck in a traffic jam as we drove across town towards the Industrial Estate. Traffic was always awful round there and today it seemed worse than usual. We sat in the queues nearly going mad as the minutes ticked by.

'I bet the meeting's already started by now,' I said.

'Don't, Claire. Be positive, please,' Mum snapped.

I'm positive the meeting's started, whispered Clarry in my stomach. 'Shut up,' I whispered back.

'Did you say something?' asked Mum.

'No.' I didn't want to say the wrong thing.

We drove past offices and warehouses and the rest till finally we arrived outside a large building with CORALS COMPUTERS on the side of it in huge lettering. Into the carpark we drove, but there was nowhere to park. Large executive-looking cars filled all the spaces. Dad's was there, parked near the building.

'It's hopeless,' I said. I'd never been to Corals Computers before, not that I'd missed much.

'We'll have to park out in the road,' said Mum, reversing out of the carpark nearly into the path of another car coming along the road. The driver wound down his window and blew his horn.

'Watch where you're going!' he bellowed.

At last we found a place to park on the other side of the road, grabbed Dad's papers and rushed into the entrance of the Corals Computers building. A receptionist was sitting behind the desk.

'Can I help you?' she asked.

'Yes. My husband's at a meeting and he's forgotten his notes,' said Mum, showing her the papers. 'It's very important.'

'I'm sorry, but the meeting has already started and I can't let you interrupt it. There are very important people here today. The Chairman and the Managing Director from Head Office, to name but two. You can wait here if you like.'

Mum found a chair and slumped into it. I joined her.

'P'raps Dad can remember his speech,' I said, trying to console her. 'After all, he read it out to you.'

'Well, I don't think he can remember the sales figures off the top of his head. He's not Troy, you know. Troy could probably memorize them if he wanted, but I don't think Dad can.'

'He might be OK anyway.'

69

'We'll have to wait and see, won't we? Keep our fingers crossed.'

About half an hour or so later a group of well-dressed men and women streamed out of the reception area. Following them was the pale, tired figure of Dad who looked years older than he had done earlier this morning.

'How did it go?' I asked. It was a stupid question looking at his face, but it came out anyway.

'How did it go? HOW DID IT GO? I arrive at one of the most important meetings of my life without my notes and you ask me that. I couldn't remember what I'd written and as for the sales figures . . .'

'You told them they were good, didn't you?' asked Mum.

'Yes, but they wanted a bit more detail than that, you know. What was I supposed to read out? Arsenal 3 Liverpool 3? I don't think they wanted Troy's football scores read out to them!'

I had a terrible feeling of wanting to laugh, but I didn't dare, not at that moment.

'We tried to catch you up,' said Mum, handing him his papers. He screwed them up and hurled them across the room. The receptionist gave him a look.

'They're no use to me now. I'm not sure if I'll still have a job here, not after this. I don't think the top brass were too impressed somehow. Let's go home. I want to get out of here for the minute.'

'Well, if the worst comes to the worst you didn't like the job anyway,' said Mum as we headed over to Dad's car.

'I'm not crazy about being sacked, though. Doesn't look good on the CV, you know. And we need the money, if you hadn't noticed.'

'Perhaps if you explained what happened . . .'

'I don't want to talk about it any more . . .'

'Well, we'll have to go back in my car now. See you back home, then.'

'If you're lucky,' I thought I heard Dad say as he climbed into his and slammed the door.

We followed Dad home, both arriving back at the same time. Troy's voice greeted us as we reached the front door.

'Have you found my scores, then?'

Dad turned round and slammed out of the house.

Chapter Nine

1 Write down phone number: 672435
2 Multiply it by two: 1344870
3 Add five to the total: 1344875
4 Multiply it by fifty: 67243750
5 Add age (9): 67243759
6 Add 365: 67244124
7 Subtract 615: 67243509

Remove the last two figures for the age 09
The rest is the phone number 672435.

Dad prowled the house like a grizzly bear with toothache, about to bite your head off to ease its pain. Then he'd slam out of the house and slam back in a few minutes later. He was as comfortable to be with as a jumping jack.

I looked at Clarry in the mirror.

'What's the matter with him?'

Dunno. But he's been like that ever since the post arrived.

Mum came in, smiling brightly, but with red eyes.

'He's lost his job. It came in the post. But he doesn't want to talk about it. I'm not sure how we shall manage now. I'll have to work full-time, I expect.'

'What about your story?'

'It's coming along quite nicely. Perhaps someone will

like it and give us loads of money. People do earn these enormous advances – thousands!'

We looked at one another. Behind me, Clarry whispered, *Not with one of your mother's stories. The* Parish Magazine *more likely!*

'What was that? You're getting very odd lately, Claire. Always talking to yourself. Try and be a bit more normal – it's bad enough with Jack always in a terrible temper . . .'

'Yeah, you're right, Mum. I'll be good. It's bad enough for you having Dad in a mood and Troy being weird . . .'

'No, no! You're wrong. Troy is OK! He's getting better all the time as he grows older. And boys are allowed to be – well – a bit different. Naughty, sometimes, but *good*, really.'

I walked away. It seemed to me that in our family Mum was really the craziest of us all.

The bell rang. I opened the door and there stood Mr Fork Bender, or whatever his name is, holding a huge bunch of roses and wearing an Armani sweatshirt and Gucci shoes – Kim tells me all about designer clothes.

'Will you please tell her, Claire, that Giles is here? I've got to see her.'

Faces appeared from all over the house – Troy peered over the banisters, Dad from the hall, Mum from the kitchen, Ness and Adam came out of her room.

'What do you want?' asked Dad, like a bulldog chewing a wasp. I don't think he likes old Fork-Bender much at the best of times, which this certainly wasn't.

'I want to see Vanessa.' He tried to push past Dad filling the doorway. 'She's been seeing me regularly until a week or so ago and I want to know what's going on.'

'I don't know what you're talking about,' said Ness, half to him, half to Adam. 'I've got my boyfriend here, standing right next to me.'

'You're talking rubbish. Vanessa hasn't been seeing you. Clear off,' said Dad.

I knew she'd been seeing him, but I wasn't about to let on. But Troy . . .

'Yes, she has,' he sang out loudly from the banisters. 'I've seen her going round to his house all dressed up.'

'Oh, shut up, you stupid little boy,' snapped Ness. 'You don't know anything apart from your rotten numbers.'

'I know about you and him, though.'

'Is this true?' demanded Adam, gazing at Ness.

'No. Well – yes. Only for a bit while you were in London. I was lonely. But when you came back, I came back to you. It didn't mean anything. It was only fun.'

'I thought we had something serious going,' cried Fortescue-Corbett.

'I'll do something serious to you in a minute,' said Dad. 'What do you think you were up to, with a girl young enough to be your daughter? There's a name for people like you!'

'She's eighteen, isn't she?'

'She's seventeen, if you want to know her exact age. Too young for you, anyway. Why can't you go out with women nearer your own age?'

'Because . . . when I saw her that time . . .'

74

'In her see-through py-jams,' called out Troy from above.

'I was smitten . . . I was in love.'

Call that love? Clarry whispered to me.

Dad's eyes were winking in an alarming way, making him look very dangerous, going off his head, cracking up, but Adam looked as if he was going to cry. Poor Adam.

'How could you, Ness? Go out with an old man like him?'

'I'm NOT an old man,' said Fortescue-C. 'I'm in the prime of life right now. And we had a good time as well. I know how to wine and dine a woman. Can you say the same? A boy like you.'

'I'm going,' said Adam to Ness. 'We're finished. If I can't trust you while I'm away for five minutes then there's no hope for our relationship.'

He stormed out of the house past Fortescue-Corbett in the doorway. For a minute I thought he was going to hit him, but instead he ran away from Thorneycroft Crescent as fast as he could go. Ness tried to follow him, but Dad stopped her. He glared at F-C.

'Just clear off right now,' he shouted. 'You've caused enough trouble today. If I hear or see you bothering Vanessa again I'm going to *knock–your–block–off*. Understand?'

'You understand nothing. I wasn't making Vanessa see me. She wanted to. We had a good time together.'

Do you think they slept together, then? whispered Clarry, in my stomach.

'Of course not. Not Ness. Shut up, Clarry.'

Maybe that same thought had come to Dad and it was just too much. He clenched his fist and sent Fortescue-Corbett sprawling down the front steps and the path, just like Troy had once done to Molly Haynes!

Must run in the family, said Clarry as F-C lay there stunned for a minute or two, then slowly got to his feet, while Dad stared, horrified at what he'd done and Ness rushed past them in the direction of where Adam had last been seen, calling, 'Adam! I love you! Wait for me!' as she flew after him down the Crescent. Heads appeared at windows, doors opened as Mr Fortescue-Corbett lurched to his feet and Dad looked ready to go for him once more. Mum and I grabbed his shirt.

'Stop it, Jack! Don't hit him again!' shrieked Mum. Then she looked at F-C. 'Vanessa doesn't want *you*. Can't you see she's in love with Adam? No, go away and stop bothering us, you silly man.'

'I'm going to bother you all right. I'm going to sue you for assault. Think you can go round hitting people when you like? Well, we'll see. There are plenty of witnesses.'

There were. Most of the Crescent was watching by now.

Better than EastEnders *or* Coronation Street, whispered Clarry, *'cos it's for real*.

'Try suing us,' laughed Dad wildly. 'The way my finances are going you're not likely to get much since I've just lost my job. And do you want to have your relationship with my daughter dragged up in court? I don't think so, somehow.'

'I've done nothing wrong! And don't think you've heard the last of this!'

F-C dusted off his Armani sweatshirt, kicked his scattered roses into the gutter and stormed off while the interested neighbourly faces watched him on his way. Bowie ran after him down the road barking loudly.

'The Spiers are horrid people,' Molly Haynes said to his mother. 'I wish they didn't live next to us.'

'I know, dear. I know. But we don't have to have anything to do with them, do we?'

Dad closed the front door away from the onlookers and then we all stood in the hall looking at each other.

'Will Ness come back? Will she be all right?' I cried.

'I don't know. Never, if she's got any sense,' said Dad. 'Julie, I'm sorry. I can't stay in this house for a minute longer. It's doing my head in. I've got to go away. Get my life sorted.'

'Does that mean we can all go on holiday?' asked Troy.

'No, I don't mean a holiday,' Dad snapped. He walked straight up to his room to pack, as Mum and I gazed at each other in shock. Then I looked at Troy.

'Why did you let on that Ness was seeing that awful man? Why couldn't you keep quiet?'

'It was true, wasn't it?'

'Well, you don't need to tell the truth all of the time, do you?'

'That's not what I've been told. I always tell the truth.'

'Yeah, that's the trouble!'

'Leave him, Claire,' said Mum. 'It's not his fault.'

It never is, is it, I thought.

Dad strode down the stairs with his suitcase. Mum grabbed his arm.

'Jack! Wait! You don't have to do this.'

'I do. I can't bear to stay here a minute longer. You know my new mobile number. Give me a call if there's an emergency or something. I don't know how long I'll be. Could be days . . . or weeks . . .'

He got into his car. Bowie ran back to him and pushed his nose inside, hoping to go walkies. Dad stroked his head, then closed the door and drove away. That was it.

He was gone.

Chapter Ten

How long is a piece of string?

And then there were three. Troy, Mum and me. And Bowie, if he counted as a person. The house seemed empty without Dad and Vanessa. Dad wrote to say that he was OK, but didn't want to come back at the moment. Mum cried and showed me the letter.

Ness had phoned up and said she was going to stay with Adam and his family for a while. She'd pop in to get her notes for A-levels and Mum wasn't to worry about her, so Mum cried again, saying she was a rotten wife and bad mother, that she couldn't do anything right and she'd always failed in everything. It seemed she'd never stop crying.

But she managed to finish her book and sent it off to an agent, hoping to hear from him soon. As money was running a bit short she went to work at the supermarket full-time. A few weeks dragged past without, amazingly, any major disaster happening until one morning Mum mentioned that the headteacher, Mrs Prentiss, wanted to see her about Troy.

'What's he done now?' I asked.

'She didn't say anything specific. She just wanted to have a general chat about him, I think.'

I don't believe you, whispered Clarry in my stomach.

79

Troy's always doing something wrong.

'Did you say something, Claire?' asked Mum.

'No. Oh, yes. Can you tell me what she says about him?'

'Of course.'

When I came in from school next day I saw Mum looking stressed and worried so I put my arms round her. It didn't seem like the interview with Mrs Prentiss went very well.

'What's happened?'

'Well, for starters – you know the exams that the school's been doing?'

'Yes, I've been doing 'em. How did I get on?'

'Oh, OK. But it's not that that matters.'

No, it wouldn't be, Clarry said, in my head.

'It's Troy. He's done exceptionally well in one subject.'

'Great! Let me guess. Maths, I suppose.'

'Yes, fairly obviously.'

'What's the problem, then?'

'Well, he's done exceptionally badly in everything else. He's filled in the answers to the questions in numbers in the other tests. His English paper was completely covered in them.'

'It was probably written in code. One of his codes.'

'Apparently he changed the letters for numbers, for example a = 1, b = 2, all the way to z = 26. But I don't think the English teacher wanted to spend his time working it out.'

'Did she say anything else about him?'

'Yes. She says he spits, swears and hits some of the other children.'

'But they're always trying to wind him up! Did you tell her that? And about Mrs Kittigrew always picking on him?'

'Yes. Then she said that she wasn't sure that he was suited to a mainstream school at all. She thinks he's got psychological problems.'

He has, muttered Clarry from my stomach.

'Shut up,' I hissed.

'Did you tell me to shut up, Claire?'

'Of course not, Mum. I'm interested in what you're saying. Have you got my results?'

'I'll tell you later. Listen. I told her that I didn't want to remove Troy from the school and she said that she'd give him another chance, but if there's any more bad behaviour then she'd have to review the situation.'

'Have you told him?'

'Yes, but I'm not sure it's sunk in. The trouble is, when he loses his temper he doesn't have any self-control. But he's a good lad, really, even if I'm the only one who thinks so.'

'I think he's good, too. Really, Mum. Now will you tell me *my* results! Please!'

They were OK. Boring really. After Troy's crazy efforts. I know I'm boring compared with Ness and Troy.

At lunchtime in school next day I walked out in the playground with Kim and my friends to see a large ring of kids gathered round two in the middle having a fight.

81

It was Troy and Molly Haynes and you couldn't really call it a fight, either. It was too one-sided for that. It was a massacre. Troy was far too strong for Molly. He was hammering him.

We got there at the same time as a teacher and Mrs Kittigrew who separated them. Molly's nose was bleeding. I think he was glad that the fight was stopped. He was taken away to see the school nurse. Troy was ordered to go and stand by the wall.

'I'm going to tell my mum what you've done,' bawled Molly as he was led away.

'You always do, you creep,' spat Troy.

'Be quiet, boy,' said Mrs Kittigrew. 'I see it's you again. You're in trouble. I'm going to inform Mrs Prentiss.'

Troy said something unprintable as she walked away.

'Oh, Troy, what have you done now?' I asked. 'Why have you beaten up Molly?'

'Because he's a sneak and I don't like him.'

'You can't go through life hitting everyone you don't like.'

'He told on me in class. I had to sit beside him and it was a really boring lesson and I was doing my numbers under the desk and he told the teacher. I worked out a marvellous number trick, but the teacher ripped it up, saying I should show proper attention in class and now I've got to work it out again from the beginning.'

Then Mrs Kittigrew returned,

'Troy Spiers, go and see the headteacher right now!'

Troy stalked away in the direction of her office.

'I'd better go with you,' I said.

'No, Claire. Mrs Prentiss wants to see him on her own,' said Mrs Kittigrew. 'This is serious.'

My friends waited with me. We stood around in a heap for centuries of time. I stuck it for about quarter of an hour, then I had to find out what was going on.

'I'm going to wait outside her office and hear what she says.'

'Do you want us to come?' asked Kim.

'No. I'd better go on my own or we'll be spotted if we all go.'

I climbed the stairs up to her office expecting to hear voices, loud voices. Instead, behind the closed door there was silence. That was strange. What was happening? I was expecting Troy to be getting a lecture but . . . nothing. I stood and waited and listened. No sound at all.

Curiosity, and Clarry egging me on were too much. I knocked and then pushed the door open. No sign of our headteacher, Mrs Prentiss. But Troy was there all right and he was busy, very, very, busy, busy, busy, busy.

There he sat on the floor surrounded by sheets of paper – test papers by the look of things. Lots and lots of them were cut into strips and scattered everywhere. A large pair of scissors – the headteacher's specials – lay beside him on the carpet with a pot of glue lying on its side and spilling over. He was sticking the strips into shapes – the one he was doing looked like the figure 8 – and he was singing one of his number songs softly to himself.

'One is one and all alone and ever more shall be so,' – that one.

He looked up at me and smiled, completely happy for once. Then he picked up a fat felt-tip pen off the floor. I saw he'd pulled all Mrs Prentiss's off her desk and they lay everywhere. He drew on the strip he was holding, up and down, round and round, up and down, over and over. His face was aglow – anyone who didn't know him might have thought he was on Ecstasy – his tiger eyes shining, his hair standing on end.

'Ness! Ness!' he shouted.

'I'm Claire – and what the heck are you doing? Are you mad? Where's Mrs Prentiss? What's happening?'

'Oh, someone fetched her for something or other. Does it matter? THIS IS WHAT MATTERS! Claire, or whoever you are, *I'VE FOUND INFINITY*!!' He drew on his bit of paper with the felt pen. 'Look, it goes on and on, round and round, up and down, on and on, round and round on this strip!'

I don't know about infinity – don't want to much. I just wanted to be out in space as Mrs Prentiss came in followed by Mrs Shepherd, the science teacher. Very slowly and carefully she breathed in and out, while I stood and trembled and Troy went on drawing with his felt pen humming, 'One is one and all alone . . .' Then she said even more very slowly and carefully, 'Troy Spiers, you are from this moment excluded from this school. Leave it immediately and go home. I shall inform your mother. If she wishes to make an appeal to the governors that is up to her. In the meantime you are excluded. Now go!'

Troy looked up. He held up his eight-like shape.

'But look! Isn't it wonderful? It's infinity!'

'Yes, it is for you. An infinity of exclusion, I hope!'

'Mrs Prentiss, please,' I cried. 'I'll clear it up for you. I'm so sorry, Mrs Prentiss, let me help.'

Frantically I tried to pick up everything, paper, scissors, glue, pens.

She ignored me.

'I want to show you . . .' Troy said, standing up.

'Just go!'

'You're making me angry!' he cried.

'That's nothing to what you're doing to me!'

Mrs Prentiss had raised her arm and pointed to the door.

'Leave the school. Go . . .'

'Please let me help . . .' I cried. She took no notice as Troy turned round and stalked out of the office, across the playground and out of the school.

As I turned to follow him, Mrs Shepherd bent down and picked up one of Troy's strips that had been stuck, but not coloured.

'Hey, look at this!'

I looked but Mrs Prentiss just glared.

'It's a Möbius strip,' she cried. 'He's been working it out all on his own! This is important.'

Mrs Prentiss sat down heavily on the one empty chair.

'I don't care what it is. I've just heard that Ofsted's coming and you know how important *that* is.'

I ran after Troy. I didn't care two pence about maths, strips and numbers. I didn't care if I was running out of school. Someone had to care for Troy and it had better be me (even if he did think I was Ness).

85

Chapter Eleven

Number Three, Number Three
Some like you, but they all like me.

When we got back to give Mum the good news (fortunately she was home) she immediately got on the phone to ask what was going on. The school secretary finally got Mrs Prentiss to phone Mum to tell her that Troy's position at the school would be reviewed at the next governors' meeting, in about a month's time. In the meantime he was excluded.

Mum then phoned Dad on his mobile to tell him what had happened and was he coming home soon? Dad said he was busy doing something at the moment, he couldn't do it at home and promised he'd be back shortly. Mum slammed down the phone, grumbling about people leaving her in the lurch and not telling her what was going on. I wanted to talk to him, but he'd switched his mobile off. It seemed lonely and miserable without him and Ness, and Mum cross and irritable all the time and Troy muttering about Mrs Prentiss being a mad woman.

But Saturday came at last and on Saturdays I usually go up town with my friends to see what we were going to buy or in my case what I would like to buy if I could. As Troy was back at home all day Mum had had to give up her job at the supermarket to look after him so we were on Social Security and claiming Income Support. Still, I quite enjoyed window shopping anyway.

We'd just come out of a music and video store when Kim said, pointing, 'Look. Isn't that Troy over there?'

'Let's see. Where?'

'Staring in that shop window at something.'

'Oh, yes. I see. Where's Mum? I thought she'd taken him out shopping with her. She doesn't like him going out on his own.'

'Is he all right?' asked Beth. 'He looks like he's in a trance or something.'

'He always looks like that,' Kim said.

Of course he's not all right, said Clarry from my middle. *He's barmy, isn't he?* I banged my stomach irritably.

'I wonder if he's going to write all over the shop window,' said Abby.

'Don't give him ideas,' I said.

'There's your mum coming this way,' said Lily.

'Hiya, Mum,' I called out. 'You looking for Troy?'

A figure laden down with shopping bags joined us.

'Yes. Where is he?'

'Over there, gazing in a window.'

'TROY,' she called. 'Come here.'

He didn't move.

'T-R-O-Y!'

A reluctant figure moved away from the window and walked over to us.

'Will you stay with me?' scolded Mum. 'I don't want to spend the morning looking for you. Let's go home.'

Since he'd been excluded, Troy wasn't especially in favour. She grabbed his arm and they went off together. I looked in the window where Troy had been, but couldn't see what he was interested in. Just loads of boxes and tins and packets of sweets and chocolates and stuff like that. I thought he'd grown out of his sweet-eating phase. Strange. Well, so was he.

'Look, there's some cool-looking clothes in there. Come on,' said Kim, looking in the shop next door, so we all trooped in there. Great. I was sick of Troy. I just wanted to think about things *we* were all interested in. *Let Mum worry about Troy*, said Clarry. *Switch off. Do your own thing.* So I did. And it was fun.

Mum was stuck at home looking after Troy so she decided to start redecorating the place partly to give her something to do and partly because if the worst happened and we had to sell the house it was a good idea to give it a makeover. So the house was full of decorating sheets, brushes, rollers, cans of paint, wallpaper, and everything was all over the place. But after a time I grew quite happy. We had some more sleepovers and my friends were in and out all the time. Mum didn't seem to mind. She'd got other things to worry about, mostly Troy. He kept slipping out and disappearing for hours, not telling her where he'd been.

One day I got home from school to find a policeman with Troy walking down the crescent to our house. Oh, no, I thought. What's he done now?

I caught them up just as the policeman rang our door-bell. Bowie answered it first, saw him holding Troy's arm and went for his trouser leg, snarling and growling. Then Mum appeared, paint-splattered, with a brush in her hand.

'Bowie! Get down!' she ordered. Bowie released the trouser leg, leaving a bite-shaped piece of cloth in his mouth.

'Is this your boy?' asked the policeman. 'He said he lived here.'

'Yes, he's mine,' sighed Mum, wearily.

'Why isn't he at school?'

'He's been excluded.'

'Well, don't you think he should be at home with you? This isn't the first time he's been out alone, is it?'

'No,' sighed Mum, more wearily.

'Don't you think it would be a good idea to keep him indoors, then? Or for you to be with him when he goes out?'

'Yes,' sighed Mum, even more wearily.

The policeman left, after talking about boy-and-dog control and damage to trousers. Mum looked more fed up and cross with Troy than I'd ever seen her before. She's always been on his side, but things were changing with Dad away.

'Right,' she said. 'Now I want to get to the bottom of this now. Why and where do you keep slipping out to?'

'I'm doing a project!'

'You're always doing projects! What project?'

'A special project!'

'What special project are you doing which involves hanging round the shopping centre for hours? You never buy anything. You could be in danger. There's some wicked people about. Mrs Haynes came round the other day and said she'd seen you there and when she told you to go home you put your tongue out and swore at her. She made some comments about people not being able to bring up their children properly. I'm tired of being called a bad mother!'

'You're not, Mum, you're not,' I cried.

Mum continued, 'If you want to go out why not ask me and we'll go together?'

'I can't do my project with you.'

'What project? Counting how many shops there are in the arcade? How many tiles there are on the floors? How many windows there are? What are you up to? You're driving me mad!'

'No, I'm not doing any of those things.'

'Matthew Taylor popped round today to say he hadn't seen Vanessa recently and was she OK, and while I was chatting to him you disappeared. I don't want to have to lock you in your room, but I might have to if this carries on. Why can't you do your number games at home? You usually like doing them. Now, when I want you to, you won't.'

'I saw him gazing in a shop window on Saturday a few days ago.' I turned to him. 'Is it something to do with that?' I asked.

'Not saying.'

'Well, why can't you help Mum decorating or take

Bowie for a walk instead of always leaving me to do it.' I tried to be helpful and ended up sounding creepy.

'Don't mention dog walking,' said Mum. 'He volunteered to do that the other day and came home hours later without him. He'd let him run round the shopping centre on his own. Heaven knows what that dog had been up to. He was looking very pleased with himself when he finally appeared. If it happens again he'll end up in the dog pound. No, I'm afraid you'll still have to do it, Claire. I can't trust him.'

'Thanks,' I said, though really I didn't mind walking Bowie.

Mum turned her attention back to Troy.

'If you don't tell me now what you're up to, I'm going to make an appointment with Dr Steele-Perkins. He's a psychiatrist. I want to know what's going on in your head.'

'What's a psych . . .?'

'A mind doctor,' I said.

The tiger eyes slitted and he trembled.

'No, Mum, please. I won't go out again. I've finished my project. Honest!'

'It's no good, Troy. Unless you tell me what you've been doing. When you were younger I thought your number games and stuff were just a phase you'd grow out of. But you're getting worse. I just can't cope with you at the moment.'

'I don't want to see a mind doctor. He'll say I'm mad. He'll lock me up with mad people. Please, Mum. Don't do it. Please.'

'He won't. They don't do that these days. He'll help you. I'm sorry, Troy. My mind's made up.'

Mum went to fetch her phone book. Troy stormed upstairs to his room. A few minutes later we poked our heads round the door. Troy was lying on the floor scribbling down numbers wildly on bits of paper, screwing them up and hurling them round the room.

'He'll see you tomorrow morning. It'll be all right. I'll come with you,' Mum said.

'Don't want to go. Don't want to see nasty doctor.'

He stayed in his room all evening, screwing up bits of paper and singing his number songs loudly over and over again until at last he fell asleep and peace came over the house.

Before I went to bed I looked at a letter left lying on the table. It said:

'I am sorry to inform you that I do not think your book is suitable for publication. I do not think it would sell in the current market.'

So Mum had been turned down. Poor Mum. Poor, poor all of us.

Next morning when I got up to go to school there was no sign of Troy. He, like Dad and Vanessa, was gone.

Chapter Twelve

Ask someone to write down any three digit number decreasing in value e.g. 6 + 4 + 2.
Write the same number backwards under the first 2 + 4 + 6 and subtract: 642 - 246 = 396.
Ask them to tell you the final digit which is 6.
You will know the remaining numbers are 3 and 9 because you subtract the 6 from the 9 to make 3 and the middle digit is always 9, no matter what three digit number was chosen.

'Mum,' I shouted down the stairs. 'Troy's not here.'
'Well, I didn't hear him go out. Have a quick look round for him. He doesn't usually go out this early.' It was eight o'clock in the morning.

So we searched the house, Bowie trying to help but getting in the way. Remembering all the places we hid in when we used to play hide-and-seek, I looked under all the beds, in the wardrobe, behind the curtains, under the stairs, cupboards, in all the chests, corners, nooks and crannies, but there was no sign of him. Then we went out into the garden and looked in the shed and the semi-jungle at the bottom. I even looked in the pond to see if he'd drowned in it, but there was only a couple of inches of water in it 'cos it had a leak and Dad hadn't fixed it yet.

'It's no good,' said Mum. 'He must've gone out. It's because he doesn't want to go to the doctor's, isn't it?'

'Yeah, I guess so,' I said. 'But I think I know where he'll be.'

I rushed straight to the island at the end of Thorneycroft Crescent with the tiny wood and the thorn bushes, Bowie alongside me. The bushes were thick and overgrown as it was summer. Troy usually hid there when he was in trouble. But he wasn't there today. I ran back home to give Mum the bad news.

'Perhaps he's gone to the shopping centre early?' I suggested.

'You could be right.'

So we jumped in Mum's car and zoomed up there. It was fairly deserted at this time of day, most of the shops not yet open. There was no sign of Troy there either.

'I've got a feeling it's going to be one of those days,' groaned Mum.

'Do you want me to miss school and help search for him?' I enquired hopefully.

'No, you go off to school,' said Mum. 'I expect he'll turn up later in the day, too late for his appointment which was supposed to be at ten o'clock. I might've guessed he'd do something like this.'

Bowie was lying on the rug in the hall like a big useless furry lump.

'Why didn't you bark or something when he went out?' I asked. 'You must have known he was going.'

He gave me a sly look and wagged his tail.

'Are you going to phone Dad and tell him?' I asked, just before I left for school.

'Only if he hasn't turned up by this evening,' she said.

'I wouldn't want to disturb his important work now, would I?'

When I got home from school at about four o'clock, Troy still hadn't turned up and Mum was beginning to get worried.

'He's never been out this long before, Claire,' she said. 'I've been to the shopping centre again and the fields where we take Bowie for his walk. There's still no sign of him. I asked at the shops if anyone had seen him and nobody had today. Do you think something might have happened to him?'

'No, Mum. He'll be hiding out somewhere. Or maybe he's still in the house.'

'I've looked everywhere, even in the loft and I hadn't been up there for ages. He's not in the house, Claire. He can't be, unless he's taken up the floorboards and is hiding underneath them. I've searched everywhere thoroughly.'

'Well, he must be out, then. P'raps he's still doing his project.'

'But why for so long? Why didn't he just come back when his appointment time was over?'

'I dunno. Have you phoned up Dad?'

'Yes. He's coming and will be here shortly. I've tried to phone Vanessa and Adam as well, but can't get any reply, which is a nuisance. We could do with all the help we need.'

'Have you phoned the police yet?'

'No. I asked Dad and he said that if we did Troy'll walk in five minutes later and we'll all look stupid.'

Well, we're used to that, aren't we? said Clarry. 'Shuddup,' I hissed.

Just at that moment the doorbell rang and in walked Dad.

'Oh, it's you,' said Mum. 'I thought it might've been Troy.'

'Sorry to disappoint you,' he said.

'I'm not disappointed. I'm very glad you're back. Oh, Jack!'

Dad looked tanned and fit, much better than I'd last seen him a couple of months before. Mum, on the other hand, looked much worse than she had a couple of months before. We all hugged each other. Bowie joined in too, leaping up and down and licking everybody.

'What's Troy been up to now, then?' asked Dad.

'He's run away and we can't find him,' I said.

'Why?'

'Because Mum wanted to send him to the mind doctor's and he didn't want to go.'

'Psychiatrist,' corrected Mum.

'We should've done that years ago. Then we might not be in this mess now,' said Dad. 'And you've looked in all the usual places, right?'

'Of course. But he's not there. He might've been . . . kidnapped . . . or something,' said Mum.

I pity the poor kidnappers if he has, said Clarry. *They've bitten off more than they can chew with him.* 'Quiet,' I hissed.

'Let's not think the worst straight away,' said Dad. 'Are there any friends' houses he might be staying at?'

'That's unlikely. He hasn't got any friends, has he?' I said. Then I got an idea.

'Perhaps he's gone to stay at Gran's by the sea.'

'No, he hasn't,' said Dad.

'How do you know?'

'Because I've been staying there.'

Mum forgot Troy for a moment and glared at him.

'Do you mean to tell me that you've spent the last few weeks relaxing and sunning yourself by the beach while I've been going through hell back here?'

'I've been working. I've told you. Gran wouldn't have let me stay with her otherwise. She'd have told me to go back home.'

'You keep saying you've been working. What have you been working on?'

'You'll see in due course. I'll tell you if it's successful.'

'You and Troy are as bad as each other. I can see where he gets his secretiveness from!'

'MUM! DAD!' I interrupted. 'This is no time to be having a row! What about Troy?'

'If he's run away because I made him go to the doctor and something's happened to him it'll be my fault. I'll always blame myself,' said Mum and burst into tears.

'I'm going to phone the police,' said Dad.

'I wanted to do that in the first place, but you said not to.'

'Oh, don't start arguing again. Not now. I'm going to have another look round,' I said.

'Good idea. I'll do that as well. Someone'll have to wait here in case he turns up and when the police come round.'

'I'll stay in,' said Mum. 'You two go and search.'

Dad jumped in his car, saying he was going to drive round the streets and look for him. I went out on foot and looked in the island again, and a couple of other places, but no joy.

I got back just as the police came round, a man and a woman. It just happened to be rotten luck that the policeman was the same one who'd brought Troy back yesterday.

'I see your little boy's missing again,' he said, keeping a wary eye on Bowie, who was being restrained by Mum. He was either wearing new trousers or had mended the ones Bowie had ripped.

'Yes,' said Mum. 'He's been gone all day.'

'And you've looked and checked everywhere? House? Friends?'

'Yes,' said Mum.

'Have you got a picture of him that we can circulate to the force and the public? Recent, if possible.'

'Yes, of course,' said Mum. She went upstairs and came down with one we'd taken on holiday.

'Nice-looking lad,' said the woman. 'Has he done this before? Run away?'

'Many times,' put in the policeman.

'He does like to go out on his own,' said Mum. 'He's never stayed out as long as this before.'

'Well, we'll keep an eye out for him. Will you inform us if he returns?'

'Yes,' said Mum. 'I'll do that first thing.'

The policeman and policewoman walked away. I thought I heard the woman say something about mothers who can't look after their kids properly and hoped this particular mother hadn't heard.

It was getting dark when Dad returned. Without Troy.

'He hasn't come back here yet, then?' he asked. 'I haven't been able to find him.'

'Noooo, he hasn't. Oh, Jack. I wish I hadn't said I was going to send him to the psychiatrist. He was scared. He thought he was going to be locked up with mad people.'

Not much different from living here, then, whispered Clarry.

'I don't think there's much more we can do tonight. It'll be too dark to see soon. I think we'll have to try again tomorrow. Let's try to get some sleep. We'll need our energy.'

'Sleep? What's sleep?' asked Mum.

Chapter Thirteen

Number Four, Number Four
Some likes enough, but I like more.

I didn't sleep very well that night and I'm sure Mum and Dad didn't either. Troy's a complete pain in the neck, but he's my brother and I love him. I couldn't bear the thought that something had happened to him, for I was starting to be afraid. My stomach wasn't talking. It hurt.

The doorbell rang. Mum opened the door immediately. But it wasn't Troy. My friends had arrived. Why had they come round today? Of course, it was Saturday, so no school today. I'd completely forgotten.

'You coming out with us?' asked Kim.

'I can't. Troy's gone missing.'

'He's done what?'

I told them all about it. Bowie rushed down the hall and started jumping up and down all around them like he does.

'You've looked everywhere, have you?' asked Kim.

'Yes, I think so.'

'Why not use Bowie? He might be able to find him.'

I looked at Bowie and wondered if he was the stupidest-looking dog in the world. Yes he was.

'It's worth a try, I s'pose,' I said doubtfully. *You hope*, Clarry muttered.

'Go and fetch something of Troy's so that Bowie gets the scent. Then take him out and see where he goes.' Kim was moving into action. Clarry went away.

So I went upstairs, fetched one of Troy's old sweaters and put it on Bowie's nose. He grabbed it and started to chew it. I tried to get it out of his mouth, but he wouldn't let go and we were having a tug-of-war in the hall when Mum came past.

'Can't you go out and look for Troy instead of playing with Bowie?' she snapped.

'I'm not playing, Mum. We're going to see if he can find him.'

'Walkies,' said Beth.

At the mention of the magic word Bowie released the sweater and ran to the door, tail wagging like crazy.

'Come on. Let's see where he takes us, then,' said Abby.

We were about to go out when Dad appeared at the door beside us.

'Where are you going?' called Mum.

'I'm going to do a house-to-house round the Crescent, asking if anybody's seen him.'

'I think the police might be doing that.'

'Well, no harm in me doing it, too. Then I'll do a drive round again. Ask some more people.'

'I'll stay in, in case there's any news,' said Mum. 'Good luck.'

'And to us,' I said.

Outside the house Bowie stopped and looked round at us, waiting for us to give him directions.

'Show him the jumper again,' said Lily.

Which I did, this time keeping it far enough away so that he couldn't grab it. He stood still, then suddenly started to trot quickly up to the end of the Crescent. We ran after him. I grabbed his lead, 'cos he wasn't very road trained.

'Look, he's on to something,' said Kim. 'Come on. Let's be the ones who find him!'

He turned quickly at the end of the road, heading upwards towards the fields. A powerful dog, he pulled me along behind him. He was on to something all right. Yeah, definitely something.

When we got to the fields I let him go, good. His lead had been biting into my hands. The fields were shaped like a 'V', high at both sides with paths, low in the middle where a stream ran along. We usually just walked Bowie along the paths, but today we'd have to go down into the fields. Troy might just be hiding in a bush or a tree or something for all we knew.

Bowie raced down the slope, the rest of us following him. It was muddy down there and my friends were all wearing quite good clothes and trainers for shopping in town.

'I'll look for him if you want,' I said. 'I don't want you to get all messed up.'

'Tough,' Kim grinned. 'We want to find Troy, don't we?'

The field Bowie chose had cows in it, surprise, surprise! He raced up to one, which lowered his head and mooed loudly. Bowie turned and fled. Then the rest of them joined in the mooing, scary, very. I slipped up and sat down in a cowpat, yucky, yuck, yuck, as we rushed after him. Next he shot down to the stream and out the other side, waiting for us, as we splashed through the six-inch-deep water till we joined him, then shook himself vigorously, spraying us generously with water. Shoes and jeans were already soaked and now our tops were wet as well. On the other side of the stream was a boggy place where all the cows walked and wallowed and Lily got stuck, so we had to pull her out minus her shoes. It took a while to rescue them. She wouldn't leave them. Said they were new, expensive and posh. They didn't look it by the time we'd retrieved them.

In the meantime Bowie had disappeared.

'Where's he gone now?' I asked.

'Behind that big bush, I think,' said Kim.

We could hear him barking, whining, whimpering and howling.

'Do you think he's found him?' cried Abby.

'He's found something. Come on, come on. COME ON!'

We rushed up to where Bowie was carrying on to find him with . . . a pretty female dog. He was rolling over, scampering, panting, showing off, cavorting, whatever you call it. The owner, a woman, was trying to get him off.

'Will you call off your dog?' she said, in a shrill tone. 'He's harassing my Sherry and he's filthy!'

I had to pull Bowie away by his collar. He wasn't very willing.

'What a waste of time,' said Beth, as if we didn't all

know. 'And I'm all mucky and messed up. Stupid dog!'

We trailed back home. No joy! No Troy!

Back home we cleaned ourselves up and grabbed some food as it was lunchtime by now. Troy still hadn't turned up, Dad was still out and Mum was waiting for news.

'What shall we do now?' asked Lily.

'Let's go to the shops. He might be there as well as anywhere,' said Abby.

'He wasn't there before,' I said.

'Well, maybe he was somewhere else before and now he's gone to the shops,' said Beth.

I didn't argue since they had spent the morning helping me look for him so we went to the shopping centre, but there was no sign of him there, and Lily kept complaining about her squelchy shoes. But as long as we were out looking for Troy, everything else didn't seem too awful. It was when you stopped that the thoughts rushed in, some Clarry's, some mine. Thoughts you didn't ever, ever want to have.

It was early evening when I came back in to find Mum, and Dad, who was back, sitting in the front room watching the telly. The local news was on.

'Is he back?' I asked, though I knew he wasn't.

'Shhh,' said Mum. 'The police have informed us that Troy is going to be mentioned on the local news. They're certainly taking it seriously.'

Then a picture of Troy flashed on the screen and the newscaster started speaking,

'It is now more than twenty-four hours since this schoolboy, Troy Spiers, was last seen, despite extensive enquiries going on. Recently there have been some cases of child abductions occurring in this region and so foul play cannot be ruled out. If anyone has any information can they contact either their local police station or ring the investigating team on this number: 72435. Thank you.'

Then the news switched over for the weather forecast.

'Well, let's hope that does the trick,' said Dad.

'Oh, Jack . . . Do you really think he's been abducted?' wailed Mum. 'I can't bear it!'

'I don't know. I don't know.'

Suddenly it was all for real. Frighteningly, sickeningly real. I ran to the loo just in time.

The phone was ringing. People were at the door. The press with cameras, friends, neighbours, teachers rang, including Mrs Prentiss. Mum took that call. I heard her shouting, 'It's all your fault!' before Dad got the phone off her.

Everyone was very sympathetic and offered to help to search for Troy. Nothing seemed real. But the one who didn't ring was Ness. We kept trying to ring her mobile, but no answer.

'Where are my children?' cried Mum. 'Where are they?'

'I'm here,' I answered, but she took no notice.

'Funny how popular you are when you're dead miserable,' Dad remarked, and then he announced, 'I'm going to the pub. I need a drink.'

'How can you think of that at a time like this?' said Mum.

'Well, I must have covered every square inch of this city today. I can't think of any road I haven't driven down. So I might as well go there, and besides, I haven't been lately. They might have seen him for all I know. It's as useful as hanging round here.'

'Can I come?' I asked, suddenly wanting to get out of the house. It was like a morgue.

'OK,' said Dad. 'I'll treat you to a lemonade and a bag of crisps.'

'Well, I'm staying here,' said Mum. 'You go and enjoy yourselves if you like.'

We slipped out of the back gate to avoid the people outside the front and ran to the pub, not far away, just behind the Crescent. As we walked in the barman greeted Jack like a long-lost friend.

'Hiya, Jack. Long time no see. Hey, I heard about your missing boy on the news. We'll all help you look for him, won't we?'

'Yes. Of course,' said the pub regulars. One of them went on, 'He's the funny lad I once found walking along the side of the railway lines, isn't he? Trying to find infinity, he said, as I brought him home.'

'Yes,' Dad answered. 'He was always trying to find infinity,' and the pub fell suddenly silent as they realized what he'd said.

I went outside to the garden to drink my lemonade as he stayed inside and chatted. It seemed weird being here without Troy. I hadn't been here without him before. And for the first time it really struck me that I might never see him again. Up till now I'd believed deep down that he was just hiding out somewhere. But now I wasn't so sure. I gulped down my lemonade quickly and ran back inside for Dad. Suddenly I didn't feel safe being on my own there any more.

That night when I went to bed I couldn't sleep properly again and lay there restlessly, tossing and turning. About midnight I heard a curious scrabbling sound nearby. I couldn't make out where it was coming from.

'That's not you, is it, Troy?' I called out. 'TROY!'

I got out of bed and ran along the landing. The light to Mum and Dad's bedroom was still on, so it looked like they were having another sleepless night. The scrabbling grew louder. What was it? I walked down the stairs into the furry form of Bowie.

'Oh, so it was you, was it?' I said. 'I thought it might've been him.'

Then I went back to bed and finally I must have slept.

And the next day was another tomorrow. And the next.

Chapter Fourteen

Choose a three digit number where all the digits are different
e.g. 752
Reverse this number (257) and subtract the smaller from the larger:
752 - 257 = 495
Reverse this number (594) and add them together:
594 + 495 = 1089
The answer is always 1089.

We sat together on the sofa, Mum and Gran and me. Beside us on a chair sat a policewoman with a collection of phones and all sorts of apparatus on a table beside her. We were watching teams of people walking, all spaced-out, over fields, beating the ground as they went, searching, searching every inch. We'd seen it all before happening to other people. But today it was us. Today belonged to Troy.

Everything was unreal.

That morning Mum and Dad had spoken on television, asking for anyone who had seen or heard or knew anything to come forward. Please, Mum had said. I'd stood near, feeling terrible. Could she do it? Would she just break down and run away (where are you, Ness, when Mum needs you?), but she was calm and spoke clearly. It was Dad who looked close to tears. It was Dad who faltered as he spoke.

After that, the information had rolled in – and I'd blanked off, as the police took over everything until we were watching the organized search, Mum and Gran and me. Dad was somewhere out there with Bowie, but we had to be on hand if needed here. Gran had come as soon as she'd heard.

Mum cried out, 'Look, there he is. There's Jack. He's with Mr Fortescue-Whatnot! He's turned out. What a surprise! He's helping to search for Troy!'

'Most of Thorneycroft Crescent's there by the look of it. And there's my teacher. And Mrs Shepherd. And nearly all of them!'

'And that's Mrs Prentiss. And Mrs Kittigrew. And so they should be. They made him run away in the first place . . .'

'Remember, Julie,' said Gran. 'Troy wasn't easy.'

'What do you mean? "Wasn't?"' cried Mum.

The word hung in the air.

'Isn't,' I said firmly. 'It isn't, Gran,' and it was then I heard Clarry say in my head, *Goodbye, Claire, you don't need me any more. You're OK on your own.* And she'd gone. No more Clarry. For a minute I was scared, then I saw Ma Haynes and Molly.

The TV camera zoomed in on them. Molly looked even more awful than usual in close-up.

'Troy was a lovely boy. He was Morris's best friend, wasn't he, Morris?'

How dare she say 'was'? I thought.

'They always played together. A dear boy. All the family are wonderful, lovely people. Morris really loved Troy, you know.'

The camera zoomed back pulling me out of misery and hate, hate.

'Why should they be the ones to speak?' I said as I looked for Kim and the girls – and there they were, plus half the school.

'People have come from miles around,' said the commentator, and tears stabbed my eyes, for it was all too much.

Gran patted me. 'I'll make a cuppa.'

'No, I'll do that,' said another policewoman. We were being well looked after.

'. . . The searchers are moving on full of determination and optimism,' concluded the commentator, zooming back to the studio.

'But I thought they all hated him,' said Gran wonderingly. 'How wrong we were.'

Much later on that endless day, we briefly saw the searchers coming back to the Crescent. Nothing had been found, no trace of clothing, nothing.

A crowd had gathered outside our house and just as we were about to join Dad and Bowie, a large purple-and-gold van drew up to our gate, scattering the crowd, causing chaos. The camera, about to zoom away, zoomed in again.

'What have we got here? Something's happening at 13 Thorneycroft Crescent. Can it be? What is it?'

A man in a gold-and-purple outfit got out, and came up to our house.

'Is this 13 Thorneycroft Crescent?'

'Yes,' cried the crowd.

By now I'd reached the door, followed by Gran and Mum. The crowd on telly and the actual crowd seemed to blur together. But I could see Dad and hear Bowie.

The man seemed surprised.

'Is this Troy Spiers' house?'

'Yes!' it was a roar this time.

'But how did you know I was coming? Is he here?'

A groan from the crowd.

The man turned to Mum.

'Are you a relative? Wife, sister, mother?'

She nodded. I could see she couldn't speak.

'Where is he, then?'

'That's what we want to know!!' the cry went up.

Dad had reached my mother and was standing beside her, holding her hand, she holding his.

'What is this?' he asked.

'I'd rather tell Troy.'

'HE ISN'T HERE!' Dad got out through gritted teeth. 'What are you messing about at?'

'Well, I suppose you'll have to do. We'll make the proper presentation later.'

'What presentation?'

'For the prize.'

'What prize?'

'For the competition.'

'What competition, for heaven's sake? I shall go mad!'

Dad was cracking up fast. He could never be patient for long.

'It's been publicized in the shopping centre for the past fortnight. Guess the number of chocky beans in the BIG GLASS JAR. Sponsored by RICH'S FAMILY CHOCKS! We do one in a different town every year with a huge prize of £10,000 for the winner!'

'Did-you-say-ten-thousand-pounds?' Dad's voice was weak.

'Yes.'

'And this has something to do with Troy, you said?'

'Troy Spiers is the winner. And I'll tell you this. You're his dad, are you, then?'

'Yes.'

'It's the first time anyone has ever guessed the exact number!! There!'

A hush had fallen over the crowd.

'Now, can I see the lucky winner? Troy? TROY!'

'Haven't you heard? He's missing. He may have been abducted. That's why all these people are here.'

There was a sighing noise like a winter wind through the trees.

'Well, I'm sorry, but I can't possibly hand over the cheque to anyone else. Keep in touch, sir. Find Troy and the ten thousand's his. But if *he* doesn't turn up the next nearest entrant will get it.'

And, whistling, the gold-and-purple man pushed his way through the crowd and drove off with a certain amount of difficulty in his gold-and-purple van.

It was nearly midnight, almost everyone had gone by now, and Thorneycroft Crescent was quiet at last. There was still no further news and we were sitting in despair when the doorbell suddenly rang. We all rushed to the door, Gran too (I was still up, Mum and Dad hadn't made me go to bed), as fast as Jack-in-the-boxes, even beating Bowie for speed.

But it wasn't Troy. Vanessa was standing there, wearing a crash helmet, Adam parking his motorbike outside. They rushed inside.

'What's going on?' she demanded, pulling off the helmet. 'What's that stupid little brother of mine been up to now? I had to cut my holiday short when I saw on the news he was missing. What's he playing at?'

'Vanessa, Vanessa, he's missing. It's been several days now. He's really gone. We've been trying to get hold of you,' cried Mum.

'Rubbish! I know him. He'll be hiding somewhere!'

'How can you say that, Vanessa?' asked Gran.

'Anyone going to let me in on what's been going on here, then?'

We gave her the full story, including the chocolate man, and we talked and talked. She and Adam had gone for a holiday to a remote village in North Wales and they hadn't heard any news for ages. When they did they headed for home as fast as possible.

At last we all fell silent. We'd said what we had to say, told all the news over and over, all of it. Then Ness gave a loud yawn and looked at the time which was half past two.

'Well, I'm off to bed. We've ridden over two hundred miles to get home and we're shattered. I still think he'll turn up somewhere. Mum, Dad, don't worry. I *know* he's OK.'

She headed up towards her bedroom. Adam drove off into the night. Then Dad said, 'Claire, you're ages past your bedtime. It's time you went up now. And us, Julie.'

'OK, Dad,' I yawned. I was having trouble keeping my eyes open.

I'd nearly reached my bedroom when a loud shriek went through the house.

'What on earth . . . ! ! ! ? ? ?'

It came from Vanessa's room. We all rushed up there to find . . .

. . . Troy lying fast asleep in her bed, looking like Sleeping Beauty.

Chapter Fifteen

Number Five, Number Five
Some likes 'em dead, but I likes 'em alive.

We all stared at Troy lying fast asleep in complete disbelief. Then Ness turned round to Mum, who looked like that picture of someone screaming. Bowie was licking him frantically, eyes shut.

'What's going on? Didn't you look for him in here, then?'

'Of course I did,' sobbed Mum. 'I looked all over the house for him several times. He can't be here! He just can't!'

'Well, he is, isn't he?'

'There's one way of finding out,' said Dad. 'Wake him up and ask him.'

Troy was still fast asleep, unaware of us in the room. Dad reached out and shook him. Hard. Troy half-opened one eye, twitched, groaned, then fell asleep again.

'It's a shame to wake him,' said Gran, sniffling.

I went up to his ear and yelled 'WAKE UP!' down it. This worked. He came to with a start to see us all looking down on him.

'Wakey-wakey,' said Dad, grinning like a gargoyle. 'You've got some explaining to do. Right now!'

'What do you all want?' asked Troy.

'Well, for a start you could tell us where you've been for the last few days.'

'I've been in a loft doing my project.'

'Not another project!'

'Yes. You know it's coming up to my birthday.'

'What's that got to do with it? Or anything?' sighed Dad

'I've been working out that only nine numbers have one digit and after that there's two or more for ever . . .'

'You've spent days working that out?' interrupted Ness.

'Oh, there's lots more to it than that . . .'

'But you *weren't* in the loft,' cried Mum. 'I looked up there. I looked everywhere in the house for you.'

'I mean next door's loft, not ours.'

'How did you get into next door's loft?'

'Through ours. If you move a bit of wood there's a gap you can squeeze through. I found it before when I was playing up there.'

'You've been next door in the Haynes's loft,' I said.

'Yeah, in their loft. And I ate some of their grub while they were out. They wouldn't notice. Molly's a greedy pig. He's always gobbling and stealing stuff. But it wasn't very comfortable to sleep up there so I came back in here for a snooze.'

'In my bed? Why my bed?' demanded Vanessa.

"Cos it's the nearest to the loft, that's why. In case I needed to get away quickly.'

'What do you need to get away quickly for, anyway?' roared Dad, temper showing as relief changed to anger.

'You were going to send me to the mind doctor. Get me locked up with mad people.'

'Not a bad idea at that,' muttered Dad.

But Mum said, 'Oh, Troy. I wasn't going to do that to you. That's not what was going to happen. They don't do that nowadays! Dr Steele-Perkins only wanted to talk to you.'

'Do you realize that half this city's been looking for you?' Dad raved. 'You've been on the news! We've been on the news! How can one person cause so much trouble?'

'Didn't you hear the crowds outside yesterday?' I asked.

'No. I was in the loft doing my numbers.'

'Good grief, if they dropped the bomb, you wouldn't notice, would you?' bellowed Dad. 'Didn't you think we'd be looking for you?'

'No. Never thought of it.'

'Don't yell at him. You'll upset him,' said Gran.

'Upset him? What do you think he does to me! What are we going to tell everybody? That he's been staying next door all the time!'

'I think you just say he'd run away and he's come back now,' said Gran.

'Yes, that would be for the best, I think,' said Mum.

Then I remembered the van.

'A man came round yesterday in a purple van saying you'd won £10,000 in a chocolate competition,' I said. 'You know anything about that?'

'Oh, yes. That was my shopping centre project. I thought I might win. I counted them for hours.'

'How could you bear to stand outside a shop for hours counting chocolate beans?' cried Ness.

'Well, I could only count some of them so I stood there working out the exact size of the bottle and how high the beans went up and the size of the beans and the number in a row and . . .'

'Don't go on,' said Dad. 'We get the picture, idiot genius.'

'I always knew he was special,' beamed Mum. 'So I'm not going to let you waste money, Troy. We'll put it in a children's account for your future.'

'I think we ought to have it,' said Ness, 'on account of all the trouble he's caused. If ever someone doesn't deserve something . . .'

'NOOOOO!' yelled Troy. 'Can't I spend any of it?'

'Well, perhaps a little for your birthday,' said Mum. 'But you're to save all the rest of it.'

'And,' said Dad, 'if you ever run away or disappear again we'll spend the rest of it. That's a promise!'

'You wouldn't,' said Troy.

'I would! I'm deadly serious. I'm not going through this again. Never. But I'd better go and inform the police and the news people that he's back.'

'Before you do that,' said Mum, 'are you going to tell me what *you've* been up to? We know what Troy's done now.'

'I'll let you know if it's successful,' said Dad.

'When?'

'I can't say exactly.'

'Well, in the meantime we need some money so I'm

going back to work in the supermarket next week. Since you're back home *you* can stay in and look after Troy!'

'OK, OK,' sighed Dad.

And so things went back to normal or as normal as they ever were in our house. Troy's return was mentioned on telly and in the local newspaper. It was never revealed where he'd really been, just that he'd run off somewhere and come back. Ma Haynes never knew that he'd been in her house and we never told her. The street and us – we were getting along fine and we wanted it to stay that way.

About a month later a letter came through the box addressed to Dad. It was from Granton Television. It said:

> We very much like the scripts you've sent us and shall be using them to make a series in due course. We shall send you the financial details later when all the matters have been finalized.

I watched as a beaming Dad showed Mum the letter.

'This is what I've been wanting to do for ages!'

'What's it all about?' asked Mum.

'A detective called Niko, who solves crime by using computers. I've had the idea for a while now.'

'Fine,' said Mum. 'As long as you write them here and not at Gran's. You can stay home and I'll go out to work. I like my job and they're going to appoint me Assistant Manager. I'm good, apparently.'

'Don't worry. I don't mind being here too much now. Troy's being fine at the moment.'

How long would that last, I thought? Until Troy's next outbreak? There'd be another before long. Life wasn't meant to be peaceful with him or anyone. But school had realized that he wasn't just crazy and awful. Mrs Shepherd said a lot about him. Good things for once, how great he was. Extra maths out of school was set up for him and every week he had to attend a class to teach him about *people* – how to talk to them, how to get on with them, how to recognize them. And he did improve. A bit.

'Send Dad,' Ness whispered to me.

She got brilliant A-Levels, took a gap year before going to Cambridge and found another boyfriend, a South American cattle millionaire. Trust Ness. Or rather don't, if you're a boy. Me, I have good friends. That's enough for me. And Troy. Dear, awful Troy. Dad's proud of him. At last. Mum always was.

'All things are numbers' – Pythagoras
   – He saw in numbers the key
   to the understanding of the Universe –

Möbius strip – a one-sided surface named after the German mathematician August Ferdinand Möbius (1790–1868). It may be formed from a long rectangular band of paper. The band is twisted in the middle through 180 degrees, and then the two ends are glued together. Such a strip has remarkable topological properties, including the fact that, unlike the original band, which is two-sided, it has only one side and one edge. If one were to start painting it from any point, the entire strip could be coloured without having to lift the brush from the surface.

Troy's fortress on the beach: he was using Pythagoras' theorem that proves the square on the hypotenuse of a right-angled triangle is equal to the sum of the squares on the other two sides.